P9-AFM-282

OUR GROUND TIME HERE WILL BE BRIEF

Maxine Kumin, who won the Pulitzer Prize in 1974 and was named Consultant in Poetry to the Library of Congress for 1981–1982, was born in Philadelphia, educated at Radcliffe College, and now lives in Warner, New Hampshire. The author of four novels, a collection of short fiction, and six volumes of poetry (including *The Retrieval System,* also published by Penguin Books), she has been a visiting professor at Washington University, Brandeis, Columbia, and elsewhere and is currently teaching at Princeton.

Also by Maxine Kumin

POETRY

Halfway
The Privilege
The Nightmare Factory
Up Country: Poems of New England
House, Bridge, Fountain, Gate
The Retrieval System

FICTION

Through Dooms of Love
The Passions of Uxport
The Abduction
The Designated Heir
Why Can't We Live Together Like Civilized Human Beings?

ESSAYS

To Make a Prairie: Essays on Poets, Poetry, and Country Living

Our Ground Time Here Will Be Brief

Maxine Kumin

PENGUIN BOOKS

PS 3521
U438
P6
1982b

PENGUIN BOOKS

Published by the Penguin Group
Viking Penguin Inc., 40 West 23rd Street, New York, New York 10010, U.S.A.
Penguin Books Ltd, 27 Wrights Lane, London W8 5TZ, England
Penguin Books Australia Ltd, Ringwood, Victoria, Australia
Penguin Books Canada Ltd, 2801 John Street,
Markham, Ontario, Canada L3R 1B4
Penguin Books (N.Z.) Ltd, 182–190 Wairau Road,
Auckland 10, New Zealand

Penguin Books Ltd, Registered Offices:
Harmondsworth, Middlesex, England

First published in the United States of America
in simultaneous hardcover and paperback editions
by Viking Penguin Inc. 1982
Reprinted 1983, 1986
Reprinted in Penguin Books 1989

10 9 8 7 6 5 4 3 2 1

Copyright © Maxine Kumin, 1957, 1958, 1959, 1960, 1961,
1962, 1963, 1964, 1965, 1970, 1971, 1972, 1973, 1974,
1975, 1976, 1977, 1978, 1979, 1980, 1981, 1982
All rights reserved

ISBN 0 14 058.643 1

Grateful acknowledgment is made to the following for permission to reprint
copyrighted material.
   Gary Snyder: A selection by Gary Snyder from *The Poet's Work*, edited by
Reginald Gibbons, published by Houghton Mifflin Company. All rights reserved.
   Viking Penguin Inc.: A selection from *Journey Around My Room: The
Autobiography of Louise Bogan* by Ruth Limmer. Copyright © Ruth Limmer,
Trustee, Estate of Louise Bogan, 1980.
   A. P. Watt Ltd and Michael and Anne Yeats: A selection from *Memoirs* by
W. B. Yeats.

Some of these poems have previously appeared in the following publications:
*Agni Review, American Poetry Review, American Review, Antaeus, Arts in Society, The
Atlantic Monthly, Audience, Berkshire Review, The Boston Review of the Arts, Boston n
University Journal, The Carleton Miscellany, Chicago Review, Crazy Horse, Denver
Quarterly, Field, Folger Shakespeare Library, Harper's, Harvard Magazine, The Hudson
Review, Inscape, Iowa Review, A Local Muse, Lynx, McCall's, Mademoiselle, The
Massachusetts Review, Missouri Review, Mother Jones, Ms., Mundus Artium, The Nation,
New American Review, New Hampshire Library Bulletin, The New Orlando Anthology,
The New Republic, The New Yorker, Ontario Review, Paintbrush, Paris Review,
Ploughshares, Poetry, The Poetry Miscellany, Poetry Northwest, Poetry Now, Quest, The
Real Paper, Saturday Review, Seattle Review, Shenandoah, TriQuarterly,* and *Tufts
Literary Quarterly.*

Except in the United States of America, this book is sold subject to the condition
that it shall not, by way of trade or otherwise, be lent, re-sold, hired out, or
otherwise circulated without the publisher's prior consent in any form of binding
or cover other than that in which it is published and without a similar condition
including this condition being imposed on the subsequent purchaser

141230

for Carole Oles   and
for William Meredith
            with gratitude for their
        sensibility and affection

and for my students, who form
a large part of the continuum

N. L. TERTELING LIBRARY
ALBERTSON COLLEGE OF IDAHO
CALDWELL, ID 83605

"Why does the struggle to come at truth take away our pity and the struggle to overcome our passions restore it again?"

—W. B. Yeats

"It is not possible, for a poet, writing in any language, to protect himself from the tragic elements in human life. . . . Illness, old age, and death—subjects as ancient as humanity—these are the subjects that the poet must speak of very nearly from the first moment that he begins to speak."

—Louise Bogan

"The *real* work is to be the warriors that we have to be, to find the heart of the monster and kill it, whether we have any hope of actually winning or not. . . . To check the destruction of the interesting and necessary diversity of life on the planet so that the dance can go on a little better for a little longer."

—Gary Snyder

Contents

Part

I.

Our Ground Time Here
Will Be Brief

Blue landing lights make
nail holes in the dark.
A fine snow falls. We sit
on the tarmac taking on
the mail, quick freight,
trays of laboratory mice,
coffee and Danish for
the passengers.

Wherever we're going
is Monday morning.
Wherever we're coming from
is Mother's lap.
On the cloud-pack above, strewn
as loosely as parsnip
or celery seeds, lie
the souls of the unborn:

my children's children's
children and their father.
We gather speed for the last run
and lift off into the weather.

Rejoicing with Henry

Not that he holds with church, but Henry goes
Christmas morning in a tantrum of snow,
Henry, who's eighty-two and has no kin
and doesn't feature prayer, but likes the singing.

By afternoon the sun is visible,
a dull gun-metal glint. We come to call
bearing a quart of home-made wine a mile
and leading Babe, our orphaned hand-raised foal.

This gladdens Henry, who stumps out to see
Babe battle the wooden bridge. Will she
or won't she? Vexed with a stick she leaps across
and I'm airborne as well. An upstate chorus
on Henry's radio renders loud
successive verses of "Joy to the World."

In spite of all the balsam growing free
Henry prefers a store-bought silver tree.
It's lasted him for years, the same
crimped angel stuck on top. Under, the same
square box from the Elks. Most likely shaving cream,
says Henry, who seldom shaves or plays the host.

Benevolent, he pours the wine. We toast
the holiday, the filly beating time
in his goat shed with her restive hooves. That's youth,
says Henry when we go to set her loose,

Never mind. Next year, if I live that long,
she'll stand in the shafts. Come Christmas Day
we'll drive that filly straight to town.
Worth waiting for, that filly. Nobody says

the word aloud: *Rejoice*. We plod
home tipsily and all uphill to boot,
the pale day fading as we go
leaving our odd imprints in the snow
to mark a little while the road
ahead of night's oncoming thick clubfoot.

Henry Manley Looks Back

Snapping kindling for the kitchen stove
Henry breaks his hip. Once he's pinned
and feeling wintry, neighbors take him in,
take in his daddy's chair, his reading lamp
—gooseneck, circa 1910— take Scamp,
his skinny whippet, in as well. Henry loves
his new life as the sage of yesteryear,
its mythic blizzards, droughts and forest fires
when he yoked oxen, killed bears, swilled applejack
and in dense snow fog brought the milk cows back
by single lantern. Meanwhile, porcupines
have entered Henry's house and set up camp.
Part of the caved-in roof now forms a ramp
for other creatures who've trooped in to raise
their young. Henry, having crutched there, says
You can't look back, and stands, bracing his spine
against the door jamb of his lost kingdom.
Scamp pokes her narrow muzzle in his palm.
The spring thaw starts, orderly and calm.

Feeding Time

Sunset. I pull on
parka, boots, mittens, hat,
cross the road to the paddock.
Cat comes,
the skinny, feral tom
who took us on last fall.
Horses are waiting.
Each enters his box
in the order they've all
agreed on, behind my back.
Cat supervises from the molding cove.
Hay first. Water next. Grain last.
Check thermometer: seven degrees.
Check latches. Leave.

The sky
goes purple, blotched with red.
Feed dog next.
I recross the road to the woodshed.
Snappish moment with cat
but no real contest.
Wag, wag, kerchunk! The plate
is polished. Dog
grovels his desire
to go inside, lie like a log
by the fire.

Two above.
Above, it's gray
with meager afterglow.
Feed birds next.
I wade by way
of footprint wells through deep snow
to cylinders on trees.
Cat follows
observing distribution
of sunflower seeds.
Checks out each heel-toe

I've stepped in, in case
something he needs,
something small and foolish lurks.
No luck.

Penultimate,
cat gets
enormous supper:
chicken gizzards! Attacks
these like a cougar
tearing, but not in haste.
Retires to barn loft
to sleep in the hay,
or pretends to. Maybe
he catches dessert this way.

Now us,
Dear One. My soup, your bread
in old blue bowls that have withstood
thirty years of slicings and soppings.
Where are the children
who ate their way through helpings
of cereals and stews
to designs of horse, pig,
sheep on view
at the bottom of the dish?
Crying, *when I grow up,*
children have got their wish.

It's ten below.
The house dozes.
The attic stringers cough.
Time that blows on the kettle's rim
waits to carry us off.

Peeling Fence Posts

Not till I hatchet a slice
the long way, slow but sure,
from the shagbark hickory
does this tough customer
shuck his warty slats
like long underwear.

The agreeable yellow birch
spooling her curls
like a typewriter ribbon
loosed from its socket
lets go in spirals,
in tendrils of neck hair

whereas, hard as it is,
ash splits its skin clean,
gives me a pry-hold,
comes away like a glove.
I finger the torso under,
pale, wet, alive.

Turning brown as a tribe
all stand leaning
together in the barrel
of oil deepened with creosote
where, in rainbow blobs
released from pith and cortex,
their tree souls float.

egret

The field's no longer simple; it's a soul's crossing time.
                                        —Roethke

All those elusive berries
that run like hen tracks
through this field of daisies
through this field of larks' nests
paintbrush, quack grass;

all those tag ends of human
speech the insects imitate
hanging their odd inflected
buzz, free-standing and misheard
in still air over this field;

all those annulled connections
all those missed chances
and time running out untested
hot and headlong like the voles'
slim tunnels in this field

running out like summer
into the mouths of immense frogs
into the blowing field and leaf clatter
calling to me and me crossing over
as if nothing were the matter.

Poem Found in the
New Hampshire Department of
Agriculture Weekly Market Bulletin

Ground saturated with water. Some
thunderstorms and wind have lodged
lots of hayland. Frost damage
in isolated pockets. From
Strafford, word of leaf miner
on beets and swiss chard. Timothy
just out of the boot and ready
to cut. Corn planting 80 per-
cent in, needs sun to green up well.
Rose chafer sighted widely, but
little sign of chewing yet.
The next few days are critical.

Thus heavily infested, June
lurches harvestward again.

the Pea Patch

These as they clack in the wind
saying castanets, saying dance with me,
saying do me, dangle their intricate
nuggety scrota

and these with the light shining through
call up a woman in a gauzy dress
young, with tendrils of hair at her neck,
leaning in a summer doorway

and as the bloom of the lime-green pod
rubs away under the polishing thumb
in the interior
sweet for the taking, nine little fetuses
nod their cloned heads.

Relearning the Language of April

Where this man walks his fences
the willows do pliés with green laces,
eyelashes fly from the white plums,
the gaunt elms begin to open their frames.

When he passes, lithe with morning,
the terriers, rump-deep in a chuckhole,
boom out to follow,
the squirrels chirrup like cardinals.

Five prick-eared ponies
lift from their serious chewing.
The doomed cattle, wearing
intelligent smiles, turn.

For miles around, the plowed fields
release a sweet rancidness
warm as sperm.

I lie in the fat lap of noon
overhearing the doves' complaint.
Far off, a stutter of geese raise alarms.

Once more, Body, Old Paint,
how could you trick me like this
in spring's blowzy arms?

Today the violets turn up blue
in the long grass as ever
a heaven can, the sea-calm color
of promises ballooning into view.
Stems long enough to lace
around your oval wrist,
small petal face
the wash of Waterman's ink,
vigilant cat's eye at the center
yellow as the sluice box where cows drink.

Today under the blue line
that covers your pulse I feel
the small purling sounds
your body makes, going on.
Time squats in the blue-spurred grass
like a yellow blister
and love in the long foreplay of spring
follows skyblue after.

Spending the Night

As bubbles are baked
into the risen loaf
so the small hot apprehension
of my death is folded in me
each time you enter my body.

Even while we hold each other
rising more surely than hornflies
to beat against the ceiling
Death tags along like a Saint Bernard
padding across his own night-alp.

Afterward I dial the grave.
My father speaks, his voice
is thin yet clear as lightning forks.
Stay home! No visitors! he calls.

While you sprawl in sleep
arms outflung like a child's
my tongue tries the salt
of this dream.
                    In the cup
of your armpit the Spoiler lurks.
Snatched out, held down, this one
time more I pass him in the dark.

ontinuum: A Love Poem

going for grapes with
ladder and pail in
the first slashing rain
of September   rain
steeping the dust
in a joyous squelch   the sky
standing up like steam
from a kettle of grapes
at the boil   wild fox grapes
wickedly high   tangled in must
of cobweb and bug spit
going for grapes   year
after year   we two with
ladder and pail stained
with the rain of grapes
our private language

Never

Good for you! he calls
beside me as I take
the chicken coop, the in-
and-out, the double oxer, all
without sucking back,
springing off my hocks
as if at Ledyard,
an Olympic champ.
Down the mud slide I whirl
clearing the drop jump,
the one my heart
lurches over, clinging
to my soft palate
where it thumps
like a snared rabbit.

O heart, we are
a pair of good girls
hurdling the ditch
at the bottom of the chute
and up the other side, *good
for you!* victorious
not over fear, my lifelong boarder,
morose skulker about the house,
but over time. The large
child inside leaps up
for daddy's loud kiss,
for daddy's lollipop.

Body on body riding hard
good for you! I play to spin
this game out to the end,
never coming to the part
where we stop,
where the jumps are set
too high, and darkness wins.

Family feeling—
even on Mount Olympus
their tongues were forked by it.
The angry sisters
tear at the paper nest
they themselves built
of tedious octagons.
The brothers line up
with longbows at
either end of the green.
The parents arise
in their graves whispering
on tiptoe lest
the neighbors hear
and a pair of pale cousins
wring their hands dry
of the whole affair.

Past clockstrike
past the last looping
of tires down the wet street
their common genes scratch
and spit. The little
familial tic jigs.
Tears throb to spill.
The dead have long since
lain back down with regret
but whoever he is
that early great-
grandfather Zeus
whose stubbornness
is yodeled from alp
to alp, awakens, watches
and rubs the ashes of lament
into his scalp.

Family Reunion

The week in August you come home,
adult, professional, aloof,
we roast and carve the fatted calf
—in our case home-grown pig, the chine
garlicked and crisped, the applesauce
hand-pressed. Hand-pressed the greengage wine.

Nothing is cost-effective here.
The peas, the beets, the lettuces
hand sown, are raised to stand apart.
The electric fence ticks like the slow heart
of something we fed and bedded for a year,
then killed with kindness's one bullet
and paid Jake Mott to do the butchering.

In winter we lure the birds with suet,
thaw lungs and kidneys for the cat.
Darlings, it's all a circle from the ring
of wire that keeps the raccoons from the corn
to the gouged pine table that we lounge around,
distressed before any of you was born.

Benign and dozy from our gluttonies,
the candles down to stubs, defenses down,
love leaking out unguarded the way
juice dribbles from the fence when grounded
by grass stalks or a forgotten hoe,
how eloquent, how beautiful you seem!

Wearing our gestures, how wise you grow,
ballooning to overfill our space,
the almost-parents of your parents now.
So briefly having you back to measure us
is harder than having let you go.

eaving My Daughter's House

I wake to the sound of horses' hooves clacking
on cobblestones, a raucous, irregular rhythm.
Mornings, the exercise boys, young Algerians
from the stable next door, take their assigned
animals into the Forêt de Soignes for a gallop.

In Belgium all such menial work is done
by Arabs or Turks. Barefoot, shivering
in the north light of 8 a.m. I stand
twitching the curtain aside to admire
the casual crouch of small men in the saddle,
their birdlike twitters, their debonair
cigarettes, and the crush of excitable horses
milling about, already lather-flecked.

I know that these skinny colts are second-rate runners.
They'll never turn up in silks at Ascot or Devon.
The closest they'll get to the ocean
is to muddy the oval track at Ostende
for the summer vacation crowd braving the drizzle
to snack on waffles or pickled eel between races.

And no matter how hard I run I know
I can't penetrate my daughter's life
in this tiny Flemish town where vectors of glass
roofs run to the horizon. Tomatoes climb
among grapes in all the greenhouses of Hoeilaart.
Although it is March, the immense purple faces
of last summer's cabbages, as if choleric
from the work of growing, still loll in the garden.

At odd hours in the rain (it is nearly
always raining) I hear the neighbor's rooster
clear-calling across the patchwork farm
where I walk among sheep the height and heft
of ponies. Their gravelly *baas* rumble
an octave lower than their American cousins.

What a Crusoe place this is, juicily rained on,
emerald-thick! What a bide-a-wee I visit
playing a walk-on part with my excursion ticket
that does not prevent my caring with secret frenzy
about this woman, this child no longer a child.

The horses are coming back now, making a calmer
metrical clatter in 4/4 time. Tomorrow
when they set out again, arching their swans' necks,
I will have crossed the ocean, gone beyond time
where we stand in a mannerly pose at the window
watching the ancient iron strike flint from stones,
balancing on the bit that links us and keeps us
from weeping o God! into each other's arms.

First waking to the gray
of linsey-woolsey cloth
the vivid spotted dogs
the red-fox cattle and
the meeker-colored horses
flattened in snow fog

first waking into gray
flecked with common cock-
crow   unfolding the same
chilblain-bruised feet
the old shoulder ache
Mama   every day

remembering how you won
the death you wished for
the death you sidled up to
remembering   how

like a child in late afternoon
drained from the jubilant sledding
you were content to coast
the run-out to a stop

booted and capped in the barn
joy enters where I haul
a hay bale by its binding string
and with my free hand pull
your easy death along.

Itinerary of an Obsession

Just remember that everything east of you has already happened.
    —*Advice on a time-zone chart*

I ascend over Paris with a planeload of pilgrims,
none under seventy, all clutching
their illustrated texts of the Holy Land
in which clouds shaped like sheep float
through the Patriarch's sky. Next to me
a little leathery woman takes out her teeth
and mines their crevices with a handkerchief.
Two nuns across the way wrap up
the dear little salt and pepper as mementos.
Pas loin, one tells me, fingering her rosary
and pointing up, when
lulled by motion or distance here you come
leaping out of the coffin again,
flapping around the funeral home
crying Surprise! I was only fooling!
while your lovesick dog chases a car
the twin of yours and lies dead
years back in a clump of goldenrod.

Later, in Rome, in St. Peter's Square
when the pope comes to the window
leaning out over his faded prayer rug
to bless the multitude, cannons are fired.
Many fall to their knees.
I have seen this before, in the rotogravure,
but not how weary the Holy Father looks
nor how frail he is, crackling into the microphone.
I am eating an orange in the static shower
of Latin when, as coolly as Pascal,
you turn up arranging to receive
extreme unction from an obliging priest
with a bad cold. You swivel your head
to keep from inhaling his germs. Pigeons
swoop past, altering the light.
I put my hands in your death
as into the carcass of a stripped turkey.

Next, on the lip of the Red Sea
in a settlement as raw as any frontier town
I meet a man from Omaha who has been detained
for nine hours at the border. They tore
the linings out of his suitcases,
they shredded his toilet kit. Tell me, he asks
from under his immense melancholy mustache,
Do I look like a terrorist? We set
out for Solomon's mines together.
In the ancient desert I stumble through mirages.
The rough red hills arouse armies of slaves,
men wasting away digging and lifting,
dying of thirst in their loincloths.
My feet weep blisters, sand enters the sores,
I bite on sand. On the floor of your closet
smolder a jumble of shoes, stiletto heels,
fleece-lined slippers, your favorite sneakers
gritty from Cape Cod, all my size.

Years pass, as they say in storybooks.
It is true that I dream of you less.
Still, when the phone rings in my sleep
and I answer, a dream-cigarette in my hand,
it is always the same. We are back at our posts,
hanging around like boxers in
our old flannel bathrobes. You haven't changed.
I, on the other hand, am forced to grow older.
Now I am almost your mother's age.
Imagine it! Did you think you could escape?
Eventually I'll arrive in her
abhorrent marabou negligee
trailing her scarves like broken promises
crying yoo-hoo! Anybody home?

Apostrophe to a Dead Friend

(on being interviewed by her biographer)

Little by little my gender drifts away
leaving the bones of this person
whose shoe size was your size
who traded dresses in our pool
of public-occasion costumes:
yours the formal-length jersey
mine the cocktail wool
and your dead mother's mink coat that
I always said looked like muskrat.

It fades, the glint of those afternoons
we lay in the sun by the pond.
Paler, the intimate confidences.
Even the distances we leapt in poems
have shrunk. No more parapets.
The men have grown smaller, drier,
easier to refuse.
Passion subsides like a sunset.
Urgency has been wrung from the rendezvous.

Now that the children have changed
into exacting adults, the warmth
we felt for each other's young
takes on the skin tone of plain daylight.
However well-fed and rosy
they are no kinder or wiser than we.

Soon I will be sixty.
How it was with you now
hardly more vivid than how
it is without you, I carry
the sheer weight of the telling
like a large infant, on one hip.
I who am remaindered in the conspiracy
doom, doom on my lips.

Bedecked with scapulars,
heavy with huge crosses
and crying out abroad,
Death to the Infidel!
the Franks swept by in waves
riding their stone horses,
big-barreled stallions
deemed brave enough for battle,

only to meet the swart,
small, mustachioed Turks
crouched nimbly athwart
their slight Arabian mares,
the only gender they
thought fit for close combat,

and thus the Rhenish stones,
running amok among
the little dish-faced mares,
the high-tailed swans-necked mares,
begetting as they went,
plunged the entire Crusade
upon the Eastern Front
into chaotic bliss.

Angels, from streets of gold,
benignly looked on this,
God's wonders to behold.
Both sides stood by unhorsed
while Nature ran its course.

IN MEMORIAM
P.W., JR.
1921–1980

The Unfinished Story

A habit I can't break, caring.
In sleep the signs come on long as a freight train.
Long as the college racing shell
he used to flip up, like an umbrella,
this brother I love, in real life shriveled
by a disease that wastes the large muscles.

Tonight he strides in rosy-cheeked
and eighteen in the pectorals
to announce he has six months to live and plans
for every hour: Pompeii, galloping
the moors at Devon, The Great Wall,
lots more sex. Further, he means to kill
time with a perpetual-motion cell.

Stickered like a housefly to the ceiling
a small watcher whispers, *this is
only a dream*. I take it, I run it through.
It is less terrible
than what I wake to.

The Incest Dream

Brother, the story's still unfinished; you
struggle up as best you can,
three-legged now as in the riddle of the Sphinx,
the whole left side of you dumb
to the brain's fiercest commands.
Talking is problematical; vowels distort
rising against the numbness in your throat.

Still, we've been out to dinner,
assorted husbands, wives,
and driving back through rain the sidewise swipe
of memory delivers a lightstruck
picture of us, ages four and six
propped in matching sailor suits
against a railing on the Boardwalk,
both wearing the family lower lip,
the family shock of hair,
two savages spruced up for Grandma's Sunday
in the roller chair.

Listen! I love you!
I've always loved you!
And so we totter and embrace
surrounded in an all-night garage
by theatergoers barking for their cars,
the obedient machines spiraling down
level by level as we block
the exit saying our good-byes,
you tangled in your cane, my black
umbrella flapping like a torn bat.

At 3 a.m. I'm driven to such extremes
that when the sorrowing hangman
brings me your severed penis still
tumescent from the scaffold
yet dried and pressed as faithfully
as a wildflower
I put it away on my closet shelf
and lie back down in my lucky shame.

Out-of-the-Body Travel

Even close to the end
when nothing works except one hand
my brother goes to the Special Cases pool
where cheerful athletes reposition
his puppet bones in a canvas sling
scoot him down the ramp
into tepid water
adjust his flotation collar
and cut him loose.

Speech has left him, but not joy.
I carry that grin
that broad important self-pleasured wink
with me into the April day.

Retrospect in the Kitchen

After the funeral I pick
forty pounds of plums from your tree
Earth Wizard, Limb Lopper
and carry them by DC 10
three thousand miles to my kitchen

and stand at midnight—nine o'clock
your time—on the fourth day of your death
putting some raveled things
unsaid between us into the boiling pot
of cloves, cinnamon, sugar.

Love's royal color
the burst purple fruit bob up.

The Man of Many L's

My whole childhood I feared cripples
and how they got that way: the one-
legged Lavender Man who sold
his sachets by St. Mary's steeple,
the blind who tapped past humming what they knew,
even the hunchback seamstress, a ragdoll
who further sagged to pin my mother's hems,
had once been sturdy, had once been whole.
Something entered people, something chopped,
pressed, punctured, had its way with them
and if you looked, bad child, it entered you.

When we found out what the disease would do,
lying, like any council's stalwarts,
all of us swore to play our parts
in the final act at your command.

The first was easy. You gave up your left hand
and the right grew wiser, a juggler for its king.
When the poor dumb leg began to falter
you took up an alpenstock for walking
once flourished Sundays by our dead father.
Month by month the battleground grew thinner.
When you could no longer swallow meat
we steamed and mashed your dinner
and bent your straw to chocolate soda treats.

And when you could not talk, still you could write
questions and answers on a magic slate,
then lift the page, like laundry to the wind.
I plucked the memory splinter from your spine
as we played at being normal, who
had eased each other in the cold zoo
of childhood. Three months before
you died I wheeled you through the streets
of placid Palo Alto to catch
spring in its flamboyant tracks.
You wrote the name of every idiot flower

I did not know. Yucca rained.
Mimosa shone. The bottlebrush took fire
as you fought to hold your great head on its stem.
Lillac, you wrote, *Magnollia. Lilly.*
And further, *olleander. Dellphinium.*

O man of many L's, brother, my wily
resident ghost, may I never spell
these crowfoot dogbane words again
these showy florid words again
except I name them under your spell.

By Heart

Dear Miss Bloomberg in your
rusty purple Eleanor Roosevelt dress
drumming your thimbled finger
on a bad child's skull
calling us up to recite one by one
from the Vision of Sir Launfal
what is so rare as a day in June?

here I stand declaiming
in that chalk-eraser-clapping clime
cowslips flutter in meadows green
when up out of the poem they come again
—marsh marigolds in proper nomenclature—
come puddling their chrome
across our still-drab wetland and pasture.

How your eyelids flutter to see the mess
of young leaves chopped and steamed
swimming in butter;
you in your Depression dress
buttoned to the chin with mother-of-pearl—
eat, eat, Miss Bloomberg! It's
spring tonic for a scurvied world.

evisiting the MacDowell Colony

The same cabin, the same stone fireplace,
red oak blazing in its sooty bin,
and just outside, October trees on fire
in the same slant of the five o'clock sun.
In the rocking chair, Louise Bogan,
girlish with company back then.
In the straight chair, theatrically puffing,
our mentor, John Holmes, with pipe.
We three novices lined up on the lumpy cot
while water was coaxed to boil over the hot
plate and jasmine tea was served in the club
they would never, o never invite us to join
who signed the plaque above the hearth
as evidence of tenancy and worth.

I strain to read above the confident fire
names of the early-great and almost-great:
Rumer Godden, Padraic Colum,
Nikolai Lopatnikoff;
too many pale ones gone to smudges.
Use a penknife, I advise my friend,
then ink each letter for relief
—as if a name might matter
against the falling leaf.

The Poets Observe the Absence of God from the St. Louis Zoo

November, that time of year the Lord
created and forgot, the big cats lurk
diminished in the mouths of their man-made caves.
Most of the pink has been bleached
from the huddled flamingos. The camels squat
over the nests of their folded legs.

To this place the aging poets, old friends,
neither quite dressed for the morning chill,
come flailing their arms in thin sunlight.
They stroll through the kingdom of roars and smells,

they shelter in the murk of the Aquarium,
peer into the mouths of ancient sea turtles,
follow the bursts of minute tropical fish
but do not raise the eternal questions:

Is utility the one criterion
for creation? Does form follow function?
Neither chooses to cite the neck
of the giraffe, the rhinoceros's horn.

Nothing is said of the opposable thumb
by means of which in the next pen a muscular
attendant in souwester and boots
force-feeds dead fish to the penguins,
cramming the smelts headfirst like grain
being tamped down the craw of a Strasbourg goose.

O *Deus absconditus,* the tamed
formal birds, glutted for the day
and balancing without shoulders, waddle
about their confines. Each of the poets
notes how helpless the natty creatures look,
how that in itself is pathetic fallacy.

They move on, arms wrapped round each other's backs.
Both are writing this poem in their heads
in a tight-lipped month between extreme weathers
while their lives speed by like outbound traffic.

Lines Written in the Library of Congress
After the Cleanth Brooks Lecture

This morning a new bird is singing
history history
time
personal identity
three
touchstones of the poem
said Mr. Brooks
almost the silver-haired last
of the Fugitives
whose books
The Well-Wrought Urn especially
poured a warm stream of wisdom
on my undergraduate past.

This morning I leave
suburban Maryland
join the warm stream
driving down the George
Washington Memorial Park
past five dead uncurled opossums
past Turkey Run
the Chain Bridge the turn-
off to Arlington's
Unknown Soldier
cross the Potomac and inch
through the bad air
of rush hour
to the identity
of my personal parking space.

Plus ça change plus
c'est la même chose.
To avoid the pestilential
slums of his people
the Sun King had
a scenic route constructed
shrubbed with roses

from Versailles to Paris.
I chat while rising
three stories
with the elevator operator
and enter this my office
coming face to face
with the architectural
miracles of
our nation's Capitol.

My door says:
CONSULTANT IN POETRY.
The hand with the arrow points here.
We live
said Mr. Brooks
in the respectable second-best
Silver Age of Literature.
I feel that at my desk.
Across it come
mannerly and rude requests
from Muse and Furies.
My job is metaphor
connotative modes of thought
irony and to introduce
the poets who read in the series.

At home in New Hampshire
the brooks are still frozen.
The barn doors
must be pickaxed loose
each morning from upheaved ground.
Evening grosbeaks cluster
in mobs at noon to devour
a spill of sunflower seed
and are gone.
Sap runs in the sugarbush
plinking from 12 to 3.
My shaggy red cows
meditate lying down
in mud under the pines.
They fatten on hay we hefted

in the sweat of late June.
Though civilization crumble
still their jaws describe
the sweet sideways munch
that works their cuds.

Down here my WATS line
relays news of failed grants
and lost petitions
from New York to California.
Two blocks away
on a gentrified street
heavy with Mercedes and pigeons
glass shatters every night
like a religion.
Thin as an eggshell the wall
crazes between Them and Us.
Newcomers live behind doors
oldtimers can kick in at will.
In a neighboring housing project
spraycan graffiti
—the script is vaguely Arabic—
announce Jesus curse Reagan
pour gall in the cup.

Meanwhile in the East Wing
of the National Gallery
Alexander
is turning into a god.
His eyes
roll up in his head.
His hair
allowed to grow into ringlets
resembles a hippie's.
He has laid waste Persepolis.
He has tramped into India.
Throughout his kingdom
the faces
of leering women look up
from the bottoms of ceremonial cups.

Everywhere lions
are being slaughtered.
Slit open
their hides are hung
on the brows of victors.
In Scythia soft gold
is spun into stalks of wheat
into acorns with pinprick pore holes.
Elaborate coins are struck
and o the horses of antiquity!
Everyman a sculptor
a poet et cetera.

Easy to attain
this cheap nostalgia
for a time as cruel as ours.
All ages are contemporaneous
Pound said
in his Golden One.
This week Pakistan
has reinstituted public floggings
with an electronic refinement:
victims wear
microphones around their necks
to amplify their screams.
In an inspired flair
one cut above reading entrails
our government rewards that regime
with military hardware.

This week Lady Bird's
two million spring bulbs
open on Capitol Hill.
My flowerbook dated 1905
says the yellow tulip
signifies hopeless love.
Magnolias
resisting lead particulates
lift their little beaks

along Pennsylvania Avenue
where triads of the unemployed
squat on the stoops
of vacant brownstones.
Angel dust is dispensed
casually in parking lots
from the front seats of old El Dorados
but to buy a *blanc de blanc*
one must enter a wineshop
barred like an arsenal.

How clumsily
I straddle these two lives!
A house guest in this city
in two weeks I go back
to lilac and apple bloom
to blackflies and caterpillars.
Morels under the apple trees.
Woodchucks. Porcupines.
The grace of mares in new pasture.
The full-time penance of mosquitoes.
Five miles of beans to hoe.
I pay fealty
to the tyranny of weather.

I pay fealty
to the wisdom of the fathers.
When I was eighteen and believed
in infinite perfectibility
I marched at Fore River
organizing the shipyard for the CIO.
Equal pay for equal work
we Cliffies chanted
meaning blacks and women
then took the subway back
to Jolly-Ups and dinners in the dorms
waited on by Irish biddies
in pale green uniforms.
Now I believe in infinite depravity.
Plus ça change. . . .

Mr. Brooks
we live suspended
between apathy and terror.
Decorum has left us.
The Silver Age tarnishes.
While the middle class
dreams of skinny dips
at Truro or the Eastern Shore
Washington slumps
in its opening heat wave.
Today in the *Post*
a respected columnist
fears new riots this summer.
Have we not
named highways and libraries
for Martin Luther King?
Called rocket sites and airports
after either Kennedy?
Weeks apart
a president and pope are shot.
The National Rifle Association
turns up its air conditioners
on Winfield Scott Circle.

Early in May in
suburban Maryland
a new bird is singing
something oracular and bright:
history history
time
running out
the bomb Mr. Brooks
in the furious grip
of the Libyans
the Iraqis Israelis Argentinians
the bomb written large
in the Domesday Book.

Poetry
makes nothing happen.

It survives
in the valley of its saying.
Auden taught us that.
Next year another
Consultant will sit
under the hand with the arrow
that props the door ajar
for metaphor.
New poets will lie on their backs
listening in the valley
making nothing happen
overhearing history
history time
personal identity
inching toward Armageddon.

From The Retrieval System

It begins with my dog, now dead, who all his long life
carried about in his head the brown eyes of my father,
keen, loving, accepting, sorrowful, whatever;
they were Daddy's all right, handed on, except
for their phosphorescent gleam tunneling the night
which I have to concede was a separate gift.

Uncannily when I'm alone these features
come up to link my lost people
with the patient domestic beasts of my life. For example,
the wethered goat who runs free in pasture and stable
with his flecked, agate eyes and his minus-sign pupils
blats in the tiny voice of my former piano teacher

whose bones beat time in my dreams and whose terrible breath
soured "Country Gardens," "Humoresque," and unplayable Bach.
My elderly aunts, wearing the heads of willful
intelligent ponies, stand at the fence begging apples.
The sister who died at three has my cat's faint chin,
my cat's inscrutable squint, and cried catlike in pain.

I remember the funeral. *The Lord is my shepherd,*
we said. I don't want to brood. Fact: it is people who fade,
it is animals that retrieve them. A boy
I loved once keeps coming back as my yearling colt,
cocksure at the gallop, racing his shadow
for the hell of it. He runs merely to be.
A boy who was lost in the war thirty years ago
and buried at sea.

Here, it's forty degrees and raining. The weatherman
who looks like my resident owl, the one who goes out and in
by the open haymow, appears on the TV screen.
With his heart-shaped face, he is also my late dentist's double,
donnish, bifocaled, kind. Going a little gray,
advising this wisdom tooth will have to come out someday,
meanwhile filling it as a favor. Another save.
It outlasted him. The forecast is nothing but trouble.
It will snow fiercely enough to fill all these open graves.

The Longing to Be Saved

When the barn catches fire
I am wearing the wrong negligee.
It hangs on me like a gunny sack.
I get the horses out, but they
wrench free, wheel, dash back
and three or four trips are required.
Much whinnying and rearing as well.
This happens whenever I travel.

At the next stopover, the children take off
their doctor and lawyer disguises
and turn back into little lambs.
They cower at windows from which flames
shoot like the tattered red cloth
of dimestore devil suits. They refuse
to jump into my waiting arms, although
I drilled them in this technique, years ago.

Finally they come to their senses and leap
but each time, the hoop holds my mother.
Her skin is as dry and papery
as a late onion. I take her
into my bed, an enormous baby
I do not especially want to keep.
Three nights of such disquiet
in and out of dreams as thin as acetate

until, last of all, it's you
trapped in the blazing fortress.
I hold the rope as you slide from danger.
It's tricky in high winds and drifting snow.
Your body swaying in space
grows heavier, older, stranger

and me in the same gunny sack
and the slamming sounds as the gutted building burns.
Now the family's out, there's no holding back.
I go in to get my turn.

ddress to the Angels

Taking off at sunset over the city
it seems we pull the sun up
and pin it over the rim
or is it the other way round,
is it the horizon we push down
like a loose cuticle?
I am up here grieving, tallying
my losses, and I think how once
the world was flat and rested on
the back of a giant fish whose tail
was in his mouth and on the Day
of Judgment all the sinners fell
overboard into the black gulf.
Once, we walked distances
or went by horse and knew our places
on the planet, gravity-wise.

Now angels, God's secret agents,
I am assured by Billy Graham,
circulate among us to tell
the living they are not alone.
On twenty-four-hour duty, angels
flutter around my house and barn
blundering into the cobwebs,
letting pots boil over
or watching the cat torture
a chipmunk. When my pony,
filching apples, rears and catches
his halter on a branch and hangs
himself all afternoon, I like
to think six equine angels fan
the strangling beast
until his agony is past.

Who knows how much or little
anyone suffers? Animals
are honest through their inability
to lie. Man, in his last hour,

has a compulsion to come clean.
Death is the sacred criterion.
Always it is passion that
confuses the issue. Always
I think that no one
can be sadder than I am.
For example, now, watching
this after after-sunset
in the sky on top of Boston
I am wanting part of my life back
so I can do it over.
So I can do it better.

Angels, where were you when
my best friend did herself in?
Were you lunching beside us
that final noon, did you catch
some nuance that went past my ear?
Did you ease my father out
of his cardiac arrest that wet
fall day I sat at the high crib bed
holding his hand? And when
my black-eyed susan-child ran
off with her European lover
and has been ever since an unbelonger,
were you whirligiging over
the suitcases? Did you put
your imprimatur on
that death-by-separation?

It's no consolation, angels,
knowing you're around
helplessly observing like
some sacred CIA. Even
if you're up here, flattened
against the Fasten Your Seatbelt sign
or hugging the bowl in the lavatory,
we are, each one of us, our own
prisoner. We are
locked up in our own story.

y Father's Neckties

Last night my color-blind chainsmoking father
who has been dead for fourteen years
stepped up out of a basement tie shop
downtown and did not recognize me.

The number he was wearing was as terrible
as any from my girlhood, a time of
ugly ties and acrimony: six or seven
blue lightning bolts outlined in yellow.

Although this was my home town it was tacky
and unfamiliar, it was Rabat or Gibraltar
Daddy smoking his habitual
square-in-the-mouth cigarette and coughing
ashes down the lightning jags. He was
my age exactly, it was wordless, a window
opening on an interior we both knew
where we had loved each other, keeping it quiet.

Why do I wait years and years to dream this outcome?
My brothers, in whose dreams he must as surely
turn up wearing rep ties or polka dots clumsily
knotted, do not speak of their encounters.

When we die, all four of us, in
whatever sequence, the designs
will fall off like face masks
and the rayon ravel from this hazy version
of a man who wore hard colors recklessly
and hid out in the foreign
bargain basements of his feelings.

Making the Connection

Looking for good news to skate out with
over the ice pond of sleep, I'm tricked instead
to think I hear him whimpering in the kitchen.
His ghost comes on metal toenails,
scratches himself, the thump of thighbone
on linoleum. Ghost laps water. Whines. Soon
he will howl in the prison of his deafness,
that paranoid, strangled sound
waking the grown children who all live elsewhere.

I sit up, breaking the connection
like hanging up on my brother.

I am ten. I go down terrified
past a houseful of bubbling breathers,
unlatch the cellar door, go further
down in darkness to lie on old carpet
next to the incontinent puppy.
His heartbeat, my heartbeat comfort us
and the fluttering pulse of the furnace
starting up, stopping, and the vague
percussion of pipes that buzz
in the far corner.

Brother,
Brother Dog, is that who you were?
Is that who I was?

The middle age you wouldn't wait
for now falls on me, white
as a caterpillar tent, white
as the sleetfall from apple trees
gone wild, petals that stick
in my hair like confetti
as I cut my way through clouds
of gnats and blackflies in the woods.

The same scarlet tanager
as last year goes up, a red
rag flagging from tree to tree,
lending a rakish permanence to
the idea of going on without you

even though my empty times
still rust like unwashed dogfood cans
and my nights fill up with porcupine
dung he drops on purpose at
the gangway to the aluminum-
flashed willow, saying that
he's been here, saying he'll come
back with his tough waddle, his pig eyes,
saying he'll get me yet. He is
the stand-in killer I use
to notarize your suicide
two years after, in deep spring.

Thomas Mann's permit to take
refuge in Switzerland said:
"for literary activities and
the passage of life's evening."
I wonder if all those he loved
and outlived showed up nights
for chips of reconstructed
dialogue under the calm Alps,
he taking both parts, working it out.

Me taking both parts in what
I suppose is my life's afternoon.

Dear friend, last night I dreamed
you held a sensitive position,
you were Life's Counselor
coming to the phone in Vaud or Bern,
some terse one-syllable place,
to tell me how to carry on

and I woke into the summer solstice
swearing I will break
your absence into crumbs
like the stump of a punky tree
working its way down
in the world's evening
down to the forest floor.

The Food Chain

The Hatchery's old bachelor, Henry Manley
backs his pickup axle-deep into my pond
opens the double tub of brookies
and begins dipping out his fingerlings.
Going in, they glint like chips of mica.

Henry waits a while to see them school up.
They flutter into clumps like living rice grains.
He leaves me some foul-smelling pellets
with instructions how to sow them on the water
a few days until they smarten and spread out.

What *he* does is shoot kingfishers with his air rifle.
They ate two thousand fry on him last weekend.
Herons? They hunt frogs, but watch for martens.
They can clean a pond out overnight.
He stands there, busy with his wrists, and looking savage.

Knowing he knows we'll hook his brookies
once they're a sporting size, I try for something
but all the words stay netted in my mouth.
Henry waves, guns the engine. His wheels spin
then catch.

Extrapolations from
Henry Manley's Pie Plant

The stalks are thick as cudgels, red
as valentines, a quarter-acre bed

planted thirty years before
Henry even toddled out of doors.

It's June. *A man of eighty-two's
too old to mow a lawn this size,* he says

meanwhile mowing. I agree, and pick.
We both know Henry's seventy-six

but people tend to brag agewise
bending the facts whatever way they choose

and the braggers-up, it seems to me,
can be forgiven the more easily.

I look at my middling self and recognize
this life is but one of a number of possible lives.

I could have studied law or medicine,
elected art history, gambled, won

or lost. I could have opened out each evening
in a downtown bar, all mirrors and singing.

Instead, mornings I commence with the sun,
tend my animals, root in the garden

and pass time with Henry. Goldfinches explode
from the meadow where thistle's the mother lode

as I follow a map no wider in landscape
than the path the wild sorrel takes.

Bearing armloads of Henry's rhubarb away,
humbly I will return him a pie or two

and when the chipmunks litter their October
feed lots with hickory husks, a home-cured

pickup full of horse manure, to let
its goodness leach out slowly in that bed

meanwhile thanking whatever's thankable
that acting on Henry's rich example

I'm to boast a hundred or so Junes
of pie plant and yellow bird and the mare's bloodlines.

The Henry Manley Blues

Henry Manley's house, unpainted for
eighty years, shrinks as attached sheds crease
and fold like paper wings. An elm tree shears
the sitting porch off in a winter storm.
And Henry's fields are going under, where
the beavers have shut down a local stream
flooding his one cash crop, neat rows of pines
he'd planned to harvest for Christmases to come.
Their tips are beanpoles now, sticking up through ice.
We skate on the newborn pond, we thump on the roof
of the lodge and squat there, listening for life.

Trouble with this country is, there's more
beavers than people in it. Henry gums
milk toast experimentally, still sore
from the painless dentist who emptied out his mouth.
Trouble is, these Conservation bums
—they're only kids, y'know, with blasting caps—
they'd rather blow the dam up than set traps,
traps is work. *By damn! They'll drive me out.*

Measurers live here, rat-shaped and tough,
with cutting tools for teeth and tails that serve
as plasterers' trowels. Where aspen's not enough
they go to birch and apple rather than starve.
Whatever tree they fell they cut the wood
in thirty-six-inch lengths. They're rarely off
that mark more than an inch or two. And what
they don't build with they store for winter food.

Henry hears their nightwork from his bed.
His phantom teeth are killing him again.
Traps! You got to trap the kit inside!
Layer by layer the lodge is packed with mud
and board by batten his view of things falls in.

Henry Manley, Living Alone, Keeps Time

Sundowning,
the doctor calls it, the way
he loses words when the light fades.
The way the names of his dear ones
fall out of his eyeglass case.
Even under the face of his father
in an oval on the wall
he cannot say *Catherine, Vera, Paul*
but goes on loving them out of place.
Window, wristwatch, cup, knife
are small prunes that drop from his pockets.
Terror sweeps him from room to room.
Knowing how much he weighed once
he knows how much he has departed his life.
Especially he knows how the soul
can slip out of the body unannounced
like that helium-filled balloon
he opened his fingers on, years back.

Now it is dark. He undresses
and takes himself off to bed
as loose in his skin as a puppy,
afraid the blankets will untuck,
afraid he will flap up, unblessed.
Instead, proper nouns return to his keeping.
The names of faces are put back
in his sleeping mouth. At first light
he gets up, grateful once more
for how coffee smells. Sits stiff
at the bruised porcelain table
saying them over, able
to with only the slightest catch.
Coffee. Coffee cup. Watch.

Birthday Poem

I am born at home
the last of four children.
The doctor brings me as promised
in his snap-jawed black leather satchel.

He takes me out in sections
fastens limbs to torso
torso to neck stem
pries Mama's navel open
and inserts me, head first.

Chin back, I swim upward
up the alimentary canal
bypassing mouth and nose holes
and knock at the top
of her head to be let out
wherefore her little bald spot.

Today my mother is eighty-two
splendidly braceleted and wigged.
She had to go four times to the well
to get me.

Changing the Children

Anger does this.
Wishing the furious wish
turns the son into a crow
the daughter, a porcupine.

Soon enough, no matter how
we want them to be happy
our little loved ones, no
matter how we prod them
into our sun that it may
shine on them, they whine
to stand in the dry-goods store.
Fury slams in.
The willful fury befalls.

Now the varnish-black son in a tree
crow the berater, denounces the race
of fathers, and the golden daughter
all arched bristle and quill
leaves scribbles on the tree bark
writing how The Nameless One
accosted her in the dark.

How put an end to this cruel spell?
Drop the son from the tree with a rifle.
Introduce maggots under his feathers
to eat down to the pure bone of boy.

In spring when the porcupine comes
all stealth and waddle to feed on the willows
stun her with one blow of the sledge
and the entrapped girl will fly out
crying Daddy! or Danny!
or is it Darling?

and we will live all in bliss
for a year and a day until
the legitimate rage of parents

speeds the lad off this time
in the uniform of a toad
who spews a contagion of warts
while the girl contracts to a spider
forced to spin from her midseam
the saliva of false repentance.

Eventually we get them back.
Now they are grown up.
They are much like ourselves.
They wake mornings beyond cure,
not a virgin among them.
We are civil to one another.
We stand in the kitchen
slicing bread, drying spoons,
and tuning in to the weather.

Each year in the after-Christmas tinsel
of the airport lounge you see them
standing like toys that have been
wound up once or twice and then
shunted aside. Mother, father,
whose bodies time has thickened
to pudding, resolute daughter,
stylish and frightened.
That small a constellation,
that commonplace a grouping.

They are done with speaking.
They do not weep.
They do not touch one another except
after the final boarding call
when they are fastened all
three as in a dangerous struggle
exploding only as she
is drawn into the silver belly of the jet
and shot from the parents
and this is the celestial arrangement.

Seeing the Bones

This year again the bruise-colored oak
hangs on eating my heart out
with its slow change, the leaves at last
spiraling end over end like your
letters home that fall Fridays
in the box at the foot of the hill
saying the old news, keeping it neutral.
You ask about the dog, fourteen years
your hero, deaf now as a turnip,
thin as kindling.

In junior high your biology class
boiled a chicken down into its bones
four days at a simmer in my pot,
then wired joint by joint
the re-created hen
in an anatomy project
you stayed home from, sick.

Thus am I afflicted, seeing the bones.
How many seasons walking
on fallen apples like pebbles in
the shoes of the Canterbury faithful
have I kept the garden up
with leaven of wood ash, kitchen leavings
and the sure reciprocation of horse dung?

How many seasons have the foals
come right or breeched or in good time
turned yearlings, two-year-olds, and at three
clattered off in a ferment to the sales?
Your ponies, those dapple-gray kings
of the orchard, long gone to skeleton,
gallop across the landscape of my dreams.
I meet my father there, dead years before
you left us for a European career.
He is looping the loop on a roller coaster
called Mercy, he is calling his children in.

I do the same things day by day.
They steady me against the wrong turn,
the closed-ward babel of anomie.
This Friday your letter in thinnest blue
script alarms me. Weekly you grow
more British with your *I shalls*
and now you're off to Africa
or Everest, daughter of the file drawer,
citizen of no return. I give
your britches, long outgrown, to the crows,
your boots with a summer visit's worth
of mud caked on them to the shrews
for nests if they will have them.

Working backward I reconstruct
you. Send me your baby teeth, some new
nail parings and a hank of hair
and let me do the rest. I'll
set the pot to boil.

Sunbathing on a Rooftop in Berkeley

Eleven palm trees stand up between me
and the Bay. A quarter turn and I'm
in line with Campanile Tower.
The hippies are sunbathing too.
They spread themselves out on the sidewalks
with their ingenious crafts for sale
and their humble puppies. We are
all pretending summer is eternal.
Mount Tamalpais hovers in the distance.

I pinch myself: that this is California!
But behind my lightstruck eyelids I am also
a child again in an amusement park
in Pennsylvania, and forty years blow
in and out adapting, as the fog does,
to conditions in the Bay.

My daughter has gone to her class in Criminal
Procedure. She pulls her hair back in a twist.
Maybe she will marry the young man she lives with?
I take note how severely
she regards the laws of search and seizure.
She moves with the assurance of a cheetah.
Still, marriage may be the sort of entrapment
she wishes to avoid? She is all uncertainties,
as I am in this mothering business.

O summers without end, the exact truth is
we are expanding sideways as haplessly
as in the mirrors of the Fun House.
We bulge toward the separate fates that await us
sometimes touching, as sleeves will, whether
or not a hug was intended.

O summers without end, the truth is
no matter how I love her, Death
blew up my dress that day
while she was in the egg unconsidered.

he Envelope

It is true, Martin Heidegger, as you have written,
I fear to cease, even knowing that at the hour
of my death my daughters will absorb me, even
knowing they will carry me about forever
inside them, an arrested fetus, even as I carry
the ghost of my mother under my navel, a nervy
little androgynous person, a miracle
folded in lotus position.

Like those old pear-shaped Russian dolls that open
at the middle to reveal another and another, down
to the pea-sized, irreducible minim,
may we carry our mothers forth in our bellies.
May we, borne onward by our daughters, ride
in the Envelope of Almost-Infinity,
that chain letter good for the next twenty-five
thousand days of their lives.

Body and Soul: A Meditation

Mornings, after leg lifts and knee bends,
I go up in a shoulder stand.
It's a form of redress. My
winter melancholy hangs
upside down. All my organs
reverse their magnetic fields:
ovaries bob on their eyestalks,
liver, kidneys, spleen, whatever
is in there functioning unseen,
free-float like parachutes,
or so it seems from Plough position,
legs behind my head, two
big toenails grazing the floor.

Body, Old Paint, Old Partner,
I ought to have paid closer
attention when Miss Bloomberg
shepherded the entire fifth grade
into the Walk-Through Woman.
I remember going
up three steps, all right,
to enter the left auricle.
I remember the violet light
which made it churchly
and the heartbeat amplified
to echo from chamber to chamber
like God speaking unto Moses.

But there was nothing about the soul,
that miners' canary flitting
around the open spaces;
no diagram in which
the little ball-bearing soul
bumbled her way downhill
in the pinball machine
of the interior, clicking
against the sternum,
the rib cage, the pelvis.

The Walk-Through Woman ceased
shortly below the waist.
Her genitals were off limits.

Perhaps there the soul
had set up housekeeping?
Perhaps a Pullman kitchen,
a one-room studio
in an erogenous zone?
O easy erogenous zones!
Flashing lights, detour
and danger signs in
the sprouting pubic hair.
Alas, I emerged from
the right ventricle
little the wiser.

Still unlocated, drifting,
my airmail half-ounce soul
shows up from time to time
like those old-fashioned
doctors who used to cheer
their patients in girls' boarding schools
with midnight bedside visits.

Body, Old Paint, Old Partner
in this sedate roundup we ride,
going up the Mountain in
the meander of our middle age
after the same old cracked tablets,
though soul and we touch tongue,

somehow it seems less sure;
somehow it seems we've come
too far to get us there.

How It Is

Shall I say how it is in your clothes?
A month after your death I wear your blue jacket.
The dog at the center of my life recognizes
you've come to visit, he's ecstatic.
In the left pocket, a hole.
In the right, a parking ticket
delivered up last August on Bay State Road.
In my heart, a scatter like milkweed,
a flinging from the pods of the soul.
My skin presses your old outline.
It is hot and dry inside.

I think of the last day of your life,
old friend, how I would unwind it, paste
it together in a different collage,
back from the death car idling in the garage,
back up the stairs, your praying hands unlaced,
reassembling the bits of bread and tuna fish
into a ceremony of sandwich,
running the home movie backward to a space
we could be easy in, a kitchen place
with vodka and ice, our words like living meat.

Dear friend, you have excited crowds
with your example. They swell
like wine bags, straining at your seams.
I will be years gathering up our words,
fishing out letters, snapshots, stains,
leaning my ribs against this durable cloth
to put on the dumb blue blazer of your death.

Splitting Wood at Six Above

I open a tree.
In the stupefying cold
—ice on bare flesh a scald—
I seat the metal wedge
with a few left-handed swipes,
then with a change of grips
lean into the eight-pound sledge.

It's muslin overhead.
Snow falls as heavy as salt.
You are four months dead.
The beech log comes apart
like a chocolate nougat.
The wood speaks
first in the tiny voice
of a bird cry, a puppet-squeak,
and then all in a rush,
all in a passionate stammer.
The papery soul of the beech
released by wedge and hammer
flies back into air.

Time will do this as fair
to hickory, birch, black oak,
easing the insects in
till rot and freeze combine
to raise out of wormwood cracks,
blue and dainty, the souls.
They are thin as an eyelash.
They flap once, going up.

The air rings like a bell.
I breathe out drops—
cold morning ghost-puffs
like your old cigarette cough.
See you tomorrow, you said.
You lied.

We're far from finished! I'm still
talking to you (last night's dream);
we'll split the phone bill.
It's expensive calling
from the other side.

Even waking it seems
logical—
your small round
stubbornly airborne soul,
that sun-yellow daisy heart
slipping the noose of its pod,
scooting over the tightrope,
none the worse for its trip,
to arrive at the other side.

It is the sound
of your going I drive
into heartwood. I stack
my quartered cuts bark down,
open yellow-face up.

It's frail, this spring snow, it's pot cheese
packing down underfoot. It flies out of the trees
at sunrise like a flock of migrant birds.
It slips in clumps off the barn roof,
wingless angels dropped by parachute.
Inside, I hear the horses knocking
aimlessly in their warm brown lockup,
testing the four known sides of the box
as the soul must, confined under the breastbone.
Horses blowing their noses, coming awake,
shaking the sawdust bedding out of their coats.
They do not know what has fallen
out of the sky, colder than apple bloom,
since last night's hay and oats.
They do not know how satisfactory
they look, set loose in the April sun,
nor what handsprings are turned under
my ribs with winter gone.

The Excrement Poem

It is done by us all, as God disposes, from
the least cast of worm to what must have been
in the case of the brontosaur, say, spoor
of considerable heft, something awesome.

We eat, we evacuate, survivors that we are.
I think these things each morning with shovel
and rake, drawing the risen brown buns
toward me, fresh from the horse oven, as it were,

or culling the alfalfa-green ones, expelled
in a state of ooze, through the sawdust bed
to take a serviceable form, as putty does,
so as to lift out entire from the stall.

And wheeling to it, storming up the slope,
I think of the angle of repose the manure
pile assumes, how sparrows come to pick
the redelivered grain, how inky-cap

coprinus mushrooms spring up in a downpour.
I think of what drops from us and must then
be moved to make way for the next and next.
However much we stain the world, spatter

it with our leavings, make stenches, defile
the great formal oceans with what leaks down,
trundling off today's last barrowful,
I honor shit for saying: We go on.

Wearing the beard of divinity, King Tut
hunts the hippopotamus of evil.
He cruises the nether world on the back
of a black leopard. And here he has put
on his special pectoral, the one
painted with granulated gold. This will
adorn him as he crosses over.

              I shuffle
in line on December seventh to see
how that royal departure took place.
A cast of thousands is passing this way.
No one looks up from the alabaster
as jets crisscross overhead. Our breaths
cloud the cases that lock in the gold
and lapis lazuli.

           The Day
of Infamy, Roosevelt called it. I was
a young girl listening to the radio
on a Sunday of hard weather. Probably
not one in seven packed in these rooms
goes back there with me.

                Implicit
throughout this exhibit arranged
by Nixon and Sadat as heads of state
is an adamantine faith
in total resurrection.
Therefore the king is conveyed
with a case for his heart
and another magnificent
hinged apparatus, far too small,
for his intestines, all in place,
all considered retrievable

whereas if one is to be blown
apart over land or water

back into the Nothingness
that precedes light, it is better
to go with the simplest detail:
a cross, a dogtag,
a clamshell.

April, in Princeton

They are moving the trees in Princeton.
Full-grown and burlapped, aboard two-ton
trucks, great larches go up the main artery
—once the retreat route of Washington's army—
to holes in the ground I know nothing of.
They are moving the trees for money and love.

They are changing the grass in Princeton
as well. They are bringing it in from sod farms
rolled tight as a church-wedding carpet, unrolled
on the lawn's raw skin in place of the old
onion grass, acid moss, dandelions.
The eye rests, approving. Order obtains.

There is no cure for beauty so replete
it hurts in Princeton. In April, here's such light
and such benevolence that winter
is overlooked, like bad table manners.
Peach, pear, and cherry bloom. The mockingbirds
seize the day, a bunch of happy drunkards

and mindful it will pass, I hurry each noon
to yoga in the Hillel Reading Room
where Yahweh and Krishna intersect in Princeton;
where, under my navel in lotus position
by sending fresh *prana* to the center
albeit lunchless, the soul may enter.

Here, let me not forget Antonin Artaud
who feared to squat, lest his immortal soul
fly out of his anus and disappear
from the madhouse in thin air.
Let me remember how I read these words
in my square white office, its windows barred

by sunlight through dust motes, my own asylum
for thoughts unsorted as to phylum.
Cerulean-blue rug softening the floor,

desk, chair, books, nothing more
except for souls aloft—Artaud's, perhaps,
and mine—drifting like the waxy cups

of white magnolias that drop their porcelain
but do not shatter, in April, in Princeton.

Late August. The goats keep leaving Eden.
Identical twin Toggenburgs, they swim
to freedom, climb tree stumps; maybe they fly?
While I boil my hands red skinning beets
their collar bells sound, distant telephones.
Intercepting the call, I go with grain
to rattle in a coffee can. One
has got an ancient pea vine in her mouth.
The other trails a plate-size bloom of squash.
When they circle me, wary but gluttonous,
I pounce, snaring one, which flops like a great warm fish
against my breasts, then stiffens, then goes limp.
I carry her off to her fenced half-acre. Meanwhile
the other, perfectly cloned, trots at my side
and interjects staccato sounds of displeasure
—at not being carried? At the genetic misfortune
of having to duplicate her sister's act?
They give me a Bronx cheer send-off, scoot
to the top of the boulder ridge, long hidden
in raspberry cane, now eaten clean, and forget
for a day or two how they came out in the world.

Late August. Truce, this instant, with what's to come.
Everything caught. This moment caught. My horse
at the paddock fence making that soft
ingratiating nicker that asks for supper.
No older and no riper than was planned
the sun staining the west. My matching hands.

July, Against Hunger

All week the rain holds off. We sweat
stuffing the barn full, like a pillow,
as much as it will hold of these
strangely dead, yellow cubes we set
in unchinked rows, so air can move between.
The smell collects, elusive, sweet,
of gray nights flecked with the snake tongue
of heat lightning, when the grownups sat
late on the side porch talking politics,
foreclosures, war, and Roosevelt.

Loneliness fills me like a pitcher.
The old deaths dribble out. My father clucks
his tongue, disapproving of manual labor.
I swivel to catch his eye, he ducks
behind the tractor, his gray fedora
melts into this year's colt munching grain.
Meanwhile, a new life kicks in the mare.
Meanwhile, the poised sky opens on rain.
The time on either side of *now* stands fast
glinting like jagged window glass.

There are limits, my God, to what I can heft
in this heat! Clearly, the Great Rat waits,
who comes all winter to gnaw on iron
or wood, and tears the last flesh from the bone.

he Survival Poem

I saw a picture of a market stall in the morning paper and under the picture was written, "The dreaded rutabaga has again made its appearance . . ." When people talk to me about the Occupation of Paris they mention the dreaded rutabaga.

—Mavis Gallant, A Fairly Good Time

Welcome, old swede,
old baggy root,
old bindrag as well
of Bonaparte's troops.
When the horses' nostrils
are webbed with ice
and out of the hay
fall torpid mice
and calves go stiff
in their mothers' wombs
and the apple core
cloaks the tunnel worm;
when the soldiers' bandages
hung out to dry
clatter like boards
in the four o'clock sky
and the last blood runs
from the bulbs of the beets
and the cabbages shed
their hundred sheets,
welcome, old swede,
strong-smelling Bigfoot.
In the camps all ate
from the same rank pot.

Let me dine with praise
on you alone.
Pray the Lord lay me down
one more time like a stone;
one winter more
from my musty bed
pray the Lord raise me up
in the morn like bread.

Notes on a Blizzard

Snow makes Monday as white
at supper as breakfast was.
All day I watch for our wild
turkeys, the ones you've tamed
with horse corn, but only the old
one comes, toeing out on his henna feet.
Small-headed, pot-bellied, he stands
too tall—I need to think this—
to tempt a raccoon. Tonight, not
turning once, I sleep in your empty space
as simply as a child in a child's cot.

Tuesday, the sky still spits
its fancywork. Wherever
the chickadees swim to is secret.
The house breathes, you occur to me as
that cough in the chimney, that phlegm-fall
while the wood fire steams, hard put
to keep itself from going out.

Wednesday, the phone's dead.
The dog coils his clay tail across
his eyes and runs, closing in
on a rabbit. Late afternoon,
in a lull, I go out on snowshoes
to look the woods over.
Above the brook a deer
is tearing bark from a birch tree,
as hungry as that, tearing
it off in strips the way
you might string celery.

Thursday, the wind turns. We're down
to snow squalls now. Last night you walked
barefoot into my dream. The mice
wrangling on all sides
raised thunder in my head,
nothing but lathe and plaster
between them and the weather.

It's Friday. The phone works.
You're driving north. Your voice
is faint, as if borne across
clothesline and tin cans from the treehouse.
The turkeys show up again
flopping under the kitchen window
like novice swimmers daring the deep end.
Low on corn, I offer jelly beans.
The sun somes out eventually,
a bedded woman, one
surprised eye open.

Territory

Mistaking him for a leaf, I cut a toad
in two with the power mower and he goes on
lopsidedly hopping until his motor runs out.

By the next pass there is no sign of my carnage.
Now I have cut a swath around the perimeter
declaring this far the grass is tamed.

I think of the wolf who marks his territory
with urine, and where there is wolf there is
the scientist who follows him, yellowing

the same pines at the same intervals
until the baffled creature, worn out
with producing urea, cedes his five acres.

We are not of it, but in it. We are
in it willynilly with our machinery
and measurements, and all for the good.

One rarely sees the blood of the toad.

How It Goes On

Today I trade my last unwise
ewe lamb, the one who won't leave home,
for two cords of stove-length oak
and wait on the old enclosed
front porch to make the swap.
November sun revives the thick
trapped buzz of horseflies. The siren
for noon and forest fires blows
a sliding scale. The lamb of woe
looks in at me through glass
on the last day of her life.

Geranium scraps from the window box
trail from her mouth, burdock burrs
are stickered to her fleece like chicken pox,
under her tail stub, permanent smears.

I think of how it goes on,
this dark particular bent of our hungers:
the way wire eats into a tree
year after year on the pasture's perimeter,
keeping the milk cows penned
until they grow too old to freshen;
of how the last wild horses were scoured
from canyons in Idaho, roped, thrown,
their nostrils twisted shut with wire
to keep them down, the mares aborting
days later, all of them carted to town.

I think of how it will be
in January, nights so cold
the pond ice cracks like target practice,
daylight glue-colored, sleet falling,
my yellow horse slick with the ball-bearing
sleet, raising up from his dingy browse
out of boredom and habit
to strip bark from the fenced-in trees;

of February, month of the hard palate,
the split wood running out,
worms working in the flour bin.

The lamb, whose time has come, goes off
in the cab of the dump truck, tied to the seat
with baling twine, durable enough
to bear her to the knife and rafter.

O lambs! The whole wolf-world sits down to eat
and cleans its muzzle after.

The Grace of Geldings in Ripe Pastures

Glutted, half asleep, browsing in
timothy grown so tall I see them
as through a pale-green stage scrim

they circle, nose to rump,
a trio of trained elephants.
It begins to rain, as promised.

Bit by bit they soak up drops
like laundry dampened to be ironed.
Runnels bedeck them. Their sides

drip like the ribs of very broad
umbrellas. And still they graze
and grazing, one by one let down

their immense, indolent penises
to drench the everlasting grass
with the rich nitrogen

that repeats them.

A Mortal Day of No Surprises

This morning, a frog in the bathtub
and not unhappy with his lot
hunkering over the downspout
out there in the pasture.
Strawberries, moreover,
but not the bearing kind, scrub
growth, many-footed pretenders,
running amok in the squash hills and valleys.

Out of here! I say
ripping the lime-green tendrils from
their pinchhold on my zucchini blossoms
and out! with a thrust of the grain scoop
to the teal-blue frog who must have fallen
from the sky in a sneakstorm that slipped
in between two and three a.m. when
even God allows for a nap.

Last night at that sneakstorm time
(God sleeping, me working out
among the old bad dreams),
two white-throated sparrows
woke me to make their departmental claims—
Old Sam Peabody peabody pea—
wrangling like clerks in adjoining bureaus
only to recommence at dawn
saying their names and territories.

Now for good measure
the dog brings in one half a rank
woodchuck no angel spoke up for
but won't say where he's banked
the rest of the treasure
and one of this year's piglets
gets loose again by rooting under,
emerging from mud like a crawfish,
to stumble across the geese's path
and have an eye pecked bloody by the gander.

All this in a summer day
to be gone like cloth at the knees
when the dark comes down
tough and ancient as thistles.
A day predictable as white-throat whistle,
a day that's indistinguishable
from thirty others, except the mare's
in heat and miserable,
squirting, rubbing her tail bare.

When I'm scooped out of here
all things animal
and unsurprised will carry on.
Frogs still will fall into those
stained old tubs we fill
with trickles from the garden hose.
Another blue-green prince will sit
like a friend of the family
guarding the doomspout.
Him asquat at the drainhole,
me gone to crumbs in the ground
and someone else's mare to call
to the stallion.

History Lesson

For Steven

You were begotten in a vague war.
American planes ran their fingers
through the sky between truces
as your daddy crossed parallels
to plant you as bald as an onion
in 1954.

Two years later you sailed
you think you remember
on a converted troopship full
of new wives and wet pants while
the plum pits of your mother's eyes
wobbled and threatened to come loose.

After that there were knots to undo
in your absent father's GI work boots
and the sounds of night robbers
cantering up the staircase
ransacking the rooming house
where you lived with your almond-eyed mother.

When they whisked her away in a bedroll
of lipstick and false eyelashes,
the landlady sent for the cops.
All the way to your first state school
a stoic, age six-and-a-half
you played games with the sergeant's handcuffs.

It is true that we lie down on cowflops
praying they'll turn into pillows.
it is true that our mothers explode
out of the snowballs of dreams
or speak to us down the chimney
saying our names above the wind.

That a man may be free of his ghosts
he must return to them like a garden.
He must put his hands in the sweet rot
uprooting the turnips, washing them
tying them into bundles
and shouldering the whole load to market.

It starts with the clothes-prop man
who is driving his stickload of notches and points
down the streets of my childhood. His horse
knocks from side to side on Lincoln Log joints
and the feedbag sways at the rear
dribbling its measure of oats.
It's the thirties again, that dream. I'm assigned
to remember laundry lifting like ghosts
on the propped-up lines where step-ins blush,
the cheeks of trousers fill, and skirts
open their petals in the washday wind.
But why just now must the horse go lame,
drop in the shafts and be left behind
struggling, struggling so to rise
that blood pours from his nose?
Why is he shot
on this Monday noon of my queer pinched life
as I watch from the parlor window seat?

Adam and Eve and Pinch Me
went down to the river to bathe.
Adam and Eve got drowneded
and who do you think got saved?

My father's bootlegger has just driven up
from Camden with a case of Cutty Sark
for the demon whiskey lovers.
My uncles move in upstairs with their beebee guns.
They're out of work.
God has a peephole even under the covers.
Squirrels fall at first light out of the pin oaks.
My brothers, short-pants man to man,
tie them in knots like old socks
and salt them away in the garbage can.
I'm the squirrel girl.
After everyone leaves for school or town
I sneak the poor burst darlings down
to the garden bed for a burial.

On the way back, muddy, I stop for a drink
at the kitchen faucet, wash up, hear
the amber bottles whistle through me clear
as scatter shot, then do
what the Almighty tells me to:
I pour my daddy's whiskey down the sink.

Adam and Eve and Pinch Me Tight
went to the movies one dark night.
Adam and Eve had an ice-cream cone
and who do you think got lost coming home?

Now I am ten. Enter Mamselle,
my mother's cut-rate milliner.
She is putting her sore eyes out in the hall
at thirty cents an hour
tacking veils onto felt forms.
Mamselle is an artist.
She can copy the Eiffel Tower
in feathers with a rolled-up brim.
She can make pyramids out of cherries.
Mamselle wears cheese boxes on her feet.
Madame can buy and sell her.
If daughters were traded among the accessories
in the perfumed hush of Bonwit Teller's
she'd have replaced me with a pocketbook,
snapped me shut and looped me over
her Hudson seal cuff; me of the chrome-wire mouth,
the inkpot braids, one eye that looks
wrongly across at the other.
O Lady of the Chaise Longue,
o Queen of the Kimono,
I disappoint my mother.

Adam and Eve and Pinch Me Flat
went to the push-nickel automat.
Adam and Eve had nickels to spend
but who do you think got left in the end?

Two more years of Kaltenborn's reports
and Poland will fall, the hearts
of horses will burst in a battle with tanks.

Soon enough the uncles will give thanks
for GI uniforms to choose
and go off tough as terriers to dig their holes.
Warsaw will excrete its last Jews.

My father will cry like a child.
He will knuckle his eyes, to my terror,
over the letters that come from the grave
begging to be sponsored, plucked up, saved.
I hoard tinfoil, meanwhile.
I knit for Britain's warriors.
This is the year that my mother stiffens.
She undresses in the closet giving me
her back as if I can't see
her breasts fall down like pufferfish,
the life gone out of their crusty eyes.
But who has punctured the bathroom light?
Why does the mattress moan at night
and why is nothing good
said of all the business to come
—the elastic belt with its metal tongue—
when my body, that surprise,
claps me into my first blood?

Adam and Eve and Pinch Me Dead
coasted down Strawberry Hill on a sled.
Adam and Eve fell off in the mud
but who do you think got covered with blood?

Sperm

You have to admire the workmanship of cousins.
There is a look in our eyes.
Once we were all seventeen of us naked as almonds.
We were all suckled except for Richard
who had to be raised on a glue of bananas.
Now he is bald and breathes through the nose
like an air conditioner but he too
said goodnight, Grandfather, when
we were all sheep in the nursery.
All of those kisses like polka dots
touched to the old man's wrinkles
while his face jittered under our little wet mouths
and he floated to the top of his palsy
sorting out Jacob from Esau.

O Grandfather, look what your seed has done!
Look what has come of those winter night gallops.
You tucking the little wife up
under the comforter that always leaked feathers.
You coming perhaps just as the trolley
derailed taking the corner at 15th Street
in a shower of blue sparks, and Grandmother's
corset spread out like a filleted fish
to air meanwhile on the window sill.
Each time a secret flourished under those laces
she eased the bones from their moorings
and swelled like the Sunday choir.
Seven sons, all with a certain
shy hood to the eye. I call it the Hummel effect.

But here, in the next generation,
I'm waiting in line at the Sedgwick
with Hester and Laura to see
Our Gang and a Shirley Temple special.
The Sedgwick has stars on the ceiling
and Shirley has banana curls.
If you have to go to the Ladies
Hester says to sit in the air

or else you will catch something awful
Hester says, even a baby.
It is Saturday. I come out in the sun
with a guilty headache while down the street
at the Lutheran Home for Incurable Orphans
a girl my age wet the bed
and stands draped in the sheets to be punished
and she could have been me.
In three years Laura will wake with
a headache that walks down her neck stem
and puts her into a wheelchair.
She grows patient as an animal.
After that I prefer not to know her.

After that, as important as summer,
the southern branch comes north to visit.
There's Sissy and Clara and Rosie
jiggling on pogo sticks, jiggling
in identical pink under-vests
while Nigger, their loyal Labrador
goes after hoptoads in the garden.
I see a brown stain on Sissy's petticoat.
I see that smart aleck, Teddy
playing games behind the furnace
with Clara. They touch in the coal bin.
He gets ten smacks with the hairbrush
and his plane goes down in the Aleutians.
Arthur's still sucking his thumb,
the same arm he loses in Italy.
Meanwhile Frederick and Ben
are born and done up in nappies.
When Frederick is sponged in the basin
and laughs, according to Rosie,
even his little beard wiggles.
Ben buttons up in the Navy
and comes home with five darling ribbons.

Such darlings, those wicked good boys
all but one come to their manhood:
Bo palming poker chips in the frat house,
Joseph gone broody with bourbon,

Michael following the horses
while nursing an early heart murmur,
Alan surprised at the Bide-A-Wee
with an upstate minister's daughter
and diffident James in the closet
trying on Sukey's garter belt,
pulling on Sukey's stockings.

O Grandfather, what is it saying,
these seventeen cousins german
descending the same number of steps
their chromosomes tight as a chain gang
their genes like innocent porters
a milk churn of spermatozoa?
You have to admire the product—
bringing forth sons to be patriots
daughters to dance like tame puppets—
half of them dead or not speaking
while Sukey and James, the end of the line,
keep house in the gentlest tradition
of spinster and bachelor sweetheart.
Memory dances me backward,
back to your dining room table
added onto to cross the front hall.
It's a squeeze play of damask on damask.
We're all wearing your hooded eyes
as you ask your aphasic blessing
over thirty-two spoons for the pudding.

he Deaths of the Uncles

I am going backward in a home movie.
The reel stutters and balks before it takes hold
but surely these are my uncles spiking the lemonade
and fanning their girls on my grandmother's veranda.
My uncles, innocent of their deaths, swatting
the shuttlecock's white tit in the Sunday twilight.
Some are wearing gray suede spats, the buttons
glint like money. Two are in checkered knickers,
the bachelor uncle in his World War One puttees
is making a mule jump for the cavalry, he is crying
Tuck, damn you, Rastus, you son of a sea cook!
How full of family feeling they are, their seven
bald heads coming back as shiny as an infection,
coming back to testify like Charlie Chaplin,
falling down a lot like Laurel and Hardy.
Stanley a skeleton rattling his closet knob
long before he toppled three flights with Parkinson's.
Everyone knew Miss Pris whom he kept in rooms
over the movie theater, rooms full of rose water
while his wife lay alone at home like a tarnished spoon.
Mitchell the specialist, big bellied, heavy of nose,
broad as a rowboat, sniffed out the spices.
Shrank to a toothpick after his heart attack,
fasted on cottage cheese, threw out his black cigars
and taken at naptime died in his dressing gown
tidy in paisley wool, old pauper thumb in his mouth.
Jasper, the freckled, the Pepsodent smiler,
cuckold and debtor, ten years a deacon
stalled his Pierce Arrow smack on a railroad track
while the twins in their pram cried for a new father.
The twins in their pram as speechless as puppies.
O run the film forward past Lawrence the baby,
the masterpiece, handsomest, favorite issue.
Cover the screen while the hats at his funeral
bob past like sailboats, like black iron cooking pots.
Larry the Lightheart dead of a bullet.
And pass over Horace, who never embezzled,
moderate Horace with sand in his eyelids

so we can have Roger again, the mule trainer
crying *son of a sea cook!* into his dotage,
wearing the Stars and Stripes next to his hearing aid,
shining his Mason's ring, fingering his Shriner's pin,
Roger the celibate, warrior, joiner

but it was Dan Dan Dan the apple of my girlhood
with his backyard telescope swallowing the stars,
with the reedy keening of his B-flat licorice stick,
Dan who took me teadancing at the Adelphia Club.
Dan who took me boating on the Schuylkill scum.
Dan who sent the roses, the old singing telegrams
and cracked apart at Normandy leaving behind
a slow-motion clip of him leading the conga line,
his white bucks in the closet and a sweet worm in my heart.

A man lies down in my mind.
We have just made love.
It went historically well, the kind
of hand-in-glove
expertise team workouts can evoke.
Now we lie still and smoke,
the ashtray on my belly blue
as chicory in the dixie cup
on the deal bureau. True,
it's a borrowed room. Third-floor walk-up
as a matter of fact,
foreign enough to enhance the act.
Say it's Grand Forks, where I've never been.
All this takes place in the head,
you understand. I play to win
back wicked afternoons in bed,
old afternoons that were
shadows on the grass longer
than home runs lofted out of the park.
We smoke. The chicory blue goes dark,
the ashtray deepens
and the sun drops
under the rim the way it happens
like a used-up lollipop
and the room goes blind
and a man
a man lies down in my mind.

Life's Work

Mother my good girl
I remember this old story:
you fresh out of the Conservatory
at eighteen a Bach specialist
in a starched shirtwaist
begging permission to go on tour
with the nimble violinist you were
never to accompany and he
flinging his music down
the rosin from his bow
flaking line by line
like grace notes on the treble clef
and my grandfather
that estimable man I never met
scrubbing your mouth with a handkerchief
saying no daughter of mine
tearing loose the gold locket
you wore with no one's picture in it
and the whole German house on 15th Street
at righteous whiteheat. . . .

At eighteen I chose to be a swimmer.
My long hair dripped through dinner
onto the china plate.
My fingers wrinkled like Sunsweet
yellow raisins from the afternoon workout.
My mouth chewed but I was doing laps.
I entered the water like a knife.
I was all muscle and seven doors.
A frog on the turning board.
King of the Eels and the Eel's wife.
I swallowed and prayed
to be allowed to join the Aquacade
and my perfect daddy
who carried you off to elope
after the fingerboard snapped
and the violinist lost his case

my daddy wearing gravy on his face
swore on the carrots and the boiled beef
that I would come to nothing
that I would come to grief. . . .

Well, the firm old fathers are dead
and I didn't come to grief.
I came to words instead
to tell the little tale that's left:
the midnights of my childhood still go on.
The stairs speak again under your foot.
The heavy parlor door folds shut
and "Clair de Lune"
puckers from the obedient keys
plain as a schoolroom clock ticking
and what I hear more clearly than Debussy's
lovesong is the dry aftersound
of your long nails clicking.

The Absent Ones

The two foals sleep back to back
in the sun like one butterfly.
Their mothers, the mares, have weaned them,
have bitten them loose like button thread.

The beavers have forced their kit
out of the stick house; he waddles
like a hairy beetle across the bottom land
in search of other arrangements.

My mother has begun to grow down,
tucking her head like a turtle.
She is pasting everyone's name
on the undersides of her silver tea service.

Our daughters and sons have burst
from the marionette show
leaving a tangle of strings
and gone into the unlit audience.

Alone I water the puffball patch.
I exhort the mushrooms to put up.
Alone I visit the hayfield.
I fork up last summer's horse-apples
to let the seeds back in the furrow.

Someone comes toward me—a shadow.
Two parts of a butterfly flicker
in false sun and knit together.
A thigh brushes my thigh.
The stones are talking in code.

I will braid up the absent ones like onions.
The missing I will wrap like green tomatoes.
I will split seventy logs for winter,
seven times seven times seven.

This is the life I came with.

The Jesus Infection

Jesus is with me
on the Blue Grass Parkway going eastbound.
He is with me
on the old Harrodsburg Road coming home.
I am listening
to country gospel music
in the borrowed Subaru.
The gas pedal
and the words
leap to the music.
O throw out the lifeline!
Someone is drifting away.

Flags fly up in my mind
without my knowing
where they've been lying furled
and I am happy
living in the sunlight
where Jesus is near.
A man is driving his polled Herefords
across the gleanings of a cornfield
while I am bound for the kingdom of the free.
At the little trestle bridge that has no railing
I see that I won't have to cross Jordan alone.

Signposts every mile exhort me
to Get Right With God
and I move over.
There's a neon message blazing
at the crossroad
catty-corner to the Burger Queen:
Ye Come With Me.
It is well with my soul, Jesus?
It sounds so easy
to be happy after the sunrise,
to be washed in the crimson flood.

Now I am tailgating
and I read a bumper sticker
on a Ford truck full of Poland Chinas.
It says: Honk If You Know Jesus
and I do it.
My sound blats out for miles
behind the pigsqueal
and it's catching in the front end,
in the axle,
in the universal joint,
this rich contagion.

We are going down the valley on a hairpin turn,
the swine and me, we're breakneck in
we're leaning on
the everlasting arms.

ving Alone with Jesus

Can it be
I am the only Jew residing in Danville, Kentucky,
looking for matzoh in the Safeway and the A & P?
The Sears, Roebuck salesman wrapping my potato masher
advises me to accept Christ as my personal saviour
or else when I die I'll drop straight down to hell,
but the ladies who come knocking with their pamphlets
say as long as I believe in God that makes us
sisters in Christ. I thank them kindly.

In the county there are thirty-seven churches
and no butcher shop. This could be taken
as a matter of all form and no content.
On the other hand, form can be seen as
an extension of content, I have read that,
up here in the sealed-off wing where my three rooms
are threaded by outdoor steps to the downstairs world.
In the open risers walnut trees are growing.
Sparrows dipped in raspberry juice
come to my one window sill. Cardinals
are blood spots before my eyes.
My bed is a narrow canoe with a fringy throw.
Whenever I type it takes to the open sea
and comes back wrong end to.
Every morning the pillows produce tapioca.
I gather it up for a future banquet.

I am leading a meatless life. I keep
my garbage in the refrigerator. Eggshells
potato peels and the rinds of cheeses nest
in the empty sockets of my daily grapefruit.
Every afternoon at five I am comforted
by the carillons of the Baptist church next door.
I let the rock of ages cleave for me on Monday.
Tuesday I am washed in the blood of the lamb.
Bringing in the sheaves on Wednesday keeps me busy.
Thursday's the day on Christ the solid rock I stand.
The Lord lifts me up to higher ground on Friday so that

Saturday I put my hands in the nail-scarred hands.
Nevertheless, I stay put on the Sabbath. I let
the whiskey bottle say something scurrilous.

Jesus, if you are in all thirty-seven churches,
are you not also here with me
making it alone in my back rooms like a flagpole sitter
slipping my peanut shells and prune pits into the Kelvinator?
Are you not here at nightfall
ticking in the box of the electric blanket?
Lamb, lamb, let me give you honey on your grapefruit
and toast for the birds to eat
out of your damaged hands.

Lately I am changing houses like sneakers and socks.
Time zones wrinkle off me casually.
I have put aside with the laundry
a row of borrowed kitchens, look-alikes
in which I crack the eggs and burn the toast
but even in Danville, Kentucky, my ghosts
come along, they relocate as easily as livestock
settling in another field. They are a dumb show
of Black Angus, and the unexpected snow
makes angels sit on their stone backs.

Angel of my cafard, displaced daughter, it was
an out-of-season snow we walked in
arms locked, two weeks ago, in the Ardennes
dreamy as soothsayers, along the Meuse
where the World War One monuments, Adonises
and sloe-eyed angels softened with verdigris,
have been updated with the names of all
those who died in labor camps
or up against the wall.
At Bastogne the wind mourned from the swamp.
A giant alarm clock ticked in the Hall
of the States, half Parthenon,
half Stonehenge, hugely American
and here I was the least at home of all
the alien places, alien beds
in the presence of my generation's dead.

This antebellum manse was built in 1836.
Sam McKee, the owner, cut his name
with a diamond on the parlor windowpane.
The glass has run with age and plays me tricks.
A stray cat overlaps my pillow again
and our cat comes back, the one named Rosencrantz,
who chose your open drawer of lollipop pants,
that cotton jumble of fruit-flavor drops,
for her first litter. She brought each forth
in a purple bubble, and ate up all the afterbirth

leaving only a damp stain in the shape
of a splayed-out frog on the top pair. Lime.
Lollipop girl, I hold back out of time
the death of your first dog gassed at the vet's
for biting one-two-three strangers single file
the one day of his life he had regrets
or maybe the one day of his true dog guile.
A stroke, they said, an insult to the brain
and I hear the lie erupt you caught me in:
he's gone to live on a farm, I said, a farm
the vet found. The dream-lie of our lives
what with the way animals come
up in everything I touch of you
and death astride them anyhow.
I told the lie that saved.

And there were turtles from the five-and-dime
carrying the fatal parasite
that ate holes in their shells, time
after time, shells growing light as lace
as one by one their hearts winked out
like the last orange eyes in the fireplace.
And this year, the new dog, the only other
dog of our days, our rootstock and our fable
now getting up backwards, the smother
of old age seizing him under the table
stuffing his ears and glazing his eyes
like great cracked aggies holding in surprise.

My arms are heavy. They hang down simian style.
I have been swimming again. I swim
to put down the cafard. The college pool
at 82 degrees is mother-warm
and the coach, a silent giant, calls me Ma'am.
He apologizes because the water is cloudy.
O my chlorinated Mediterranean! Hold me!
I rock across that cradle, a shipwreck
for twenty laps, then haul myself on deck
back in the impossible freight of my body.

Body that housed you, but now claims no right
except in the snapshot on the window ledge
of a borrowed parlor where a diamond bit
the glass to save a man's name from the dark.
It's last summer in this picture, a day on the edge
of our time zone. We are standing in the park,
our genes declare themselves, death smiles in the sun
streaking the treetops, the sky all lightstruck. . . .
In the dark you were packed about with toys,
you were sleeping on your knees, never alone,
your breathing making little o's
of trust, night smooth as soapstone
and the hump of your bottom like risen bread. . . .

Darling, Belgian citizen, I put away my dread
but things knock at the elephant legs of this house.
In the bump of pipes there thunders the horse
who kicked you in the face the year you were eleven.
The welt on your cheek raised up round and even
as a biscuit, and we had no ice, but put
a block of frozen meat to it. Still
I see the scar come up in certain lights
when you're at the window, thin as a pencil.

Let the joists of this house endure their dry rot.
Let termites push under them in their blind tunnels
thoughtfully chewing. I chew on the knot
we were once. Meanwhile, your eyes, serene
in the photo, look most thoughtfully out
and could be bullet holes, or beauty spots.

To Swim, to Believe

Centre College, Danville, Kentucky

The beautiful excess of Jesus on the waters
is with me now in the Boles Natatorium.
This bud of me exults, giving witness:

these flippers that rose up to be arms.
These strings drawn to be fingers.
Legs plumped to make my useful fork.

Each time I tear this seam to enter,
all that I carry is taken from me,
shucked in the dive.

Lovers, children, even words go under.
Matters of dogma spin off in the freestyle
earning that mid-pool spurt, like faith.

Where have I come from? Where am I going?
What do I translate, gliding back and forth
erasing my own stitch marks in this lane?

Christ on the lake was not thinking
where the next heel-toe went.
God did him a dangerous favor

whereas Peter, the thinker, sank.

The secret is in the relenting,
the partnership. I let my body work

accepting the dangerous favor
from this king-size pool of waters.
Together I am supplicant. I am bride.

he Selling of the Slaves

Lexington, Kentucky

The brood mares on the block at Tipton Pavilion
have ears as delicate as wineglass stems.
Their eyes roll up and out like china dolls'.
Dark red petals flutter in their nostrils.
They are a strenuous ballet, the thrust and suck
of those flanks, and meanwhile the bags of foals
joggle, each pushing against its knapsack.

They are brought on one at a time, worked over
in the confines of a chain-link silver tether
by respectful attendants in white jackets
and blackface. The stage manager hovers
in the background with a gleaming shovel
and the air ripens with the droppings he dips up.

In the velvet pews a white-tie congregation
fans itself with the order of the service.
Among them pass the prep-school deacons
in blazers and the emblems of their districts.
Their hymnals are clipboards. The minister
in an Old Testament voice recites
a liturgy of bloodlines. Ladies and Gentlemen:

Hip Number 20 is Rich and Rare
a consistent and highclass producer.
She is now in foal to that good horse, Brazen.
Candy Dish slipped twins on January one
and it is with genuine regret I must announce
that Roundabout, half sister to a champion,
herself a dam of winners, is barren this season.

She is knocked down at eleven thousand dollars
to the man from Paris with a diamond in his tooth,
the man from Paris with a snake eye in his collar.

When money changes hands among men of worth
it is all done with sliding doors and decorum
but snake whips slither behind the curtain.
In the vestry flasks go round. The gavel's
report is a hollow gunshot:
sold, old lady! and the hot
manure of fear perfumes God's chapel.

...airing the Geese on
...ly Forty-Ninth Birthday

The gosling's eye is lidless
and navy blue.
A series of shutters clicks in it.
Yellow flecks, like plankton,
swim over the flutter.
I, who am in fact new
to this business, look in
on the morning of June six
and see my own pale embryo
chipping away with its egg tooth.

The gosling's sex is deeply kept.
Under its feathers
a sort of button lurks.
I squeeze around it as if
to open a pimple
and expose a shy, two-way conduit,
a male-female look-alike
tunnel of nursery pink
except the penis, if one is intended,
will pop up in it.

My other hand, meanwhile,
strokes the gosling's breast
to keep it sootheful on its back
while being sexed.
These are my birthday birds,
gift from a neighbor's hatch.

We kneel to our work, agreeing
it's demeaning but not cruel.
Six birds later, each squirting upward,
feces dribbling on my shirt, her shirt,
the unmistakable gander stands forth.

How mildly each one permits
this upending!

Head on a swivel, it watches.
Its docked wings lie down
like elbow stumps so that
my goslings, once I've paired them,
will not flap up from the pond
where they've been planted
to decorate the surface,
to honk with their white trumpets,
to come, in the slippage of my days,
of mating age,
preening each other's feathers,
eating each other's lice.

The parsnips, those rabbis
have braided their beards together
to examine the text. The word
that engrosses them is: February.

To be a green tomato
wrapped in the Sunday book section
is to know nothing. Meanwhile
the wet worm eats his way outward.

These cabbages, these clean keepers
in truth are
a row of impacted stillbirths.
One by one we deliver them.

O potato, a wink of
daylight and you're up with
ten tentative erections.
How they deplete you!

Dusty blue wart hogs, the squash
squat for a thump and a tuning.
If we could iron them out
they'd be patient blue mandolins.

The beets wait wearing their birthmarks.
They will be wheeled into the amphitheater.
Even before the scrub-up, the scalpel,
they bleed a little.

I am perfect, breathes the onion.
I am God's first circle
the tulip that slept in His navel.
Bite me and be born.

Insomnia

To hear the owl is the poet's prerogative.

In the hand-me-down of dead hours
I hear him moving up the mountain
tree by tree insistent as
a paranoid calling out his one verse
raising the break-bone alarm like
those quaint East European churches
that tolled their non-Sunday bells
to usher in the pogrom.

Finally he settles in my basswood.
We both doze listening for each other.
Going out to help my horse up
in the first light I see him
hurry into the haymow
furtive as an old boarder
flapping along the corridor
to tell his secret to the toilet.

O red eye! Sit tight
up in the rafters.
Hang on
safe as a puffball.
Tonight
another chapter—
the promise of hatchets.

Two nights running I was out there
in orange moonlight with old bedsheets
and a stack of summered-over Sunday papers
tucking up the tomatoes while the peppers
whimpered and went under and the radishes
dug in with their dewclaws and all over
the field the goldenrod blackened
and fell down like Napoleon's army.

This morning they're still at it, my tomatoes
making marbles, making more of those little
green volunteers that you can rattle
all winter in a coat pocket, like fingers.
But today on the lip of the solstice
I will pull them, one hundred
big blind greenies. I will stand them
in white rows in the root cellar
wrapped one by one
in the terrible headlines.

On Digging Out Old Lilacs

I stand in a clump of dead athletes.
They have been buried upright
in Olympic poses. One
a discobolus clutching a bird's nest.
One a runner trailing laces of snakeskin.
One a boxer exploding toads of cracked leather.

I call in the hatchet, the mattock, the crowbar
the dog with his tines, for
the trick is to get at the taproot.
Each one is as thick as a weightlifter's thigh.

First you must rupture those handholds but
each has a stone in its fist.
Each one encloses beetles that pinch
like aroused crabs. Some
will not relax even when
bludgeoned about the neckbone.

Next you must chip up kneecaps and scapulas.
Knuckles and hammertoes fly in the dustbin
until on my hands and knees
I ring something metal. An ox shoe
hatched underground for a hundred years
a gristle of earth in its mouth.

I see them at the pasture wall
the great dumb pair
imperfectly yoked and straining
straining at the stone boat and
meanwhile the shoe in my hand
its three prongs up on the half-moon.

It is enough that the lilacs must go,
a mess of broken bones in the gully.
I give the shoe back to the earth
for now I am a woman
in a long-gone dooryard
flinging saved dishwasher onto
these new slips.

Let it end with the goat
carrying his ears
like empty cornucopias
the goat still stripping brush
after the blight of frost
or when the blanket comes down
debarking logs in the woodpile.
Goat a factory of himself
a fermentation vat
spilling the beebee shot wastes
out of the basket of his rectum
goat the survival artist.

Song for Seven Parts of the Body

I.

This one,
a common type,
turns in.
Was once attached.
Fed me as sweetly
as an opium pipe.
O, birthdays unlimber us,
eyes sit back,
ears go indoors,
but here nothing changes.
This was.
This is.

II.

Mostly they lie low
put up shells, sprout hairs
and if they sing, they know
only leather cares.
Blind marchers five abreast
left, right
silent as mushrooms or puff paste
they rise up free at night.

III.

I have a life of my own
he says. He is transformed
without benefit of bone.
I will burrow, he says
and enters. Afterwards
he goes slack as a slug.
He remembers little.
The prince is again a frog.

IV.

Here is a field that never lies fallow.
Sweat waters it, nails hoe the roots.

Every day death comes in with the winnow.
Every day newborns crop up like asparagus.
At night, all night on the pillow
you can hear the narrow sprouts crackle
rubbing against each other,
lying closer than lemmings.
They speak to their outposts in armpits.
They speak to their settlers in crotches.
Neighbor, neighbor, they murmur.

v.

They have eyes that see not.
they straddle the valley of wishes.
Their hills make their own rules.
Among them are bobbers
melons, fishes
doorknobs and spools.
At times they whisper, touch me.

VI.

Imagine a mouth
without you, pink man,
goodfellow.
A house
without a kitchen,
a fishless ocean.
No way to swallow.

VII.

These nubbins
these hangers-on
hear naught.
Wise men
tug them in thought.
Lovers
may nibble each other's
Maidens
gypsies and peasants
make holes in theirs
to hang presents.

The Eternal Lover

The last grasshoppers
thinner than pick-up sticks
breast up out of the goldenrod.
They know they are flying into
the end of the journey.
Toads in their outsize skins
doze on stones,
taking what they can get.
Meanwhile the woodchuck
is dragging his rusty heartbeat
deep under the granite ledges.
He will be dreamless all winter.

The lover, shaving,
consults his mirror.
Last night's dream stands behind him
all teeth and mouth and legs.
For twenty years he has lain
with legions of golden girls
alike as polka dots
each with a butterfly mouth
to be planted under his tongue.
He sips from the plastic champagne glass.
He has much to consider.
It is that season for him too.

Meanwhile Mother on Elm Street
verboten in her corset
can be seen lying on the rooftop
can be seen hammering down the shingles
can be seen spilling out the honey
can be seen savaging the carpet.
In one frame she cries clumsily
her tears loose as gumdrops
her mouth pulled down like a rubber band.

Meanwhile he is required
to make ineffectual love to

his first girl over and over
the Jessie, the joy of his hometown.
He undresses her under the bleachers.
Armed to the teeth with entreaties
he replays that fearsome scrimmage
of buttons and bra straps and stockings
dreaming the same dream the same dream

while grasshoppers rise in the tall weeds
to take their last lap in the pasture
like cross-country hurdlers.

Running Away Together

It will be an island on strings
well out to sea and austere
bobbing as if at anchor
green with enormous fir trees
formal as telephone poles.

We will arrive there slowly
hand over hand without oars.
Last out, you will snip the fragile
umbilicus white as a beansprout
that sewed us into our diaries.

We will be two bleached hermits
at home in our patches and tears.
We will butter the sun with our wisdom.
Our days will be grapes on a trellis
perfectly oval and furred.

At night we will set our poems
adrift in ginger ale bottles
each with a clamshell rudder
each with a piggyback spider
waving them off by dogstar

and nothing will come from the mainland
to tell us who cares, who cares
and nothing will come of our lovelock
except as our two hearts go soft
and black as avocado pears.

eaven as Anus

In the Defense Department there is a shop
where scientists sew the eyelids of rabbits open
lest they blink in the scorch of a nuclear drop

and elsewhere dolphins are being taught to defuse
bombs in the mock-up of a harbor and monkeys
learn to perform the simple tasks of draftees.

It is done with electric shocks. Some mice
who have failed their time tests in the maze
now go to the wire unbidden for their jolts.

Implanting electrodes yields rich results:
alley cats turn from predators into prey.
Show them a sparrow and they cower

while the whitewall labs fill up with the feces of fear
where calves whose hearts have been done away
with walk and bleat on plastic pumps.

And what is any of this to the godhead,
these squeals, whines, writhings, unexpected jumps,
whose children burn alive, booby-trap the dead,
lop ears and testicles, core and disembowel?

It all ends at the hole. No words may enter
the house of excrement. We will meet there
as the sphincter of the good Lord opens wide
and He takes us all inside.

Young Nun at Bread Loaf

Sister Elizabeth Michael
has come to the Writers' Conference.
She has white habits like a summer sailor
and a black notebook she climbs into nightly
to sway in the hammock of a hundred knotted poems.
She is the youngest nun I have ever known.

When we go for a walk in the woods
she puts on a dimity apron that teases her boottops.
It is sprigged with blue flowers.
I wear my jeans and sneakers. We are looking
for mushrooms (chanterelles are in season)
to fry and eat with my drinks, her tomato juice.

Wet to the shins with crossing
and recrossing the same glacial brook, a mile
downstream we find them, the little pistols,
denser than bandits among the tree roots.
Forager, she carries the basket.
Her hands are crowded with those tough yellow thumbs.

Hiking back in an unction of our own sweat
she brings up Christ. Christ, that canard!
I grind out a butt and think of the waiting bourbon.
The sun goes down in disappointment.
You can say what you want, she says.
You live as if you believe.

Sister
Sister Elizabeth Michael
says we are doing Christ's work, we two.
She, the rosy girl in a Renoir painting.
I, an old Jew.

the Uneasy Sleep of the Translator

With a broad shoehorn
I am unstuffing a big bird in this dream
—somebody else's holiday feast—
and repacking the crop of my own,
knowing it will burst with such
onion, oyster, savory bread crust.

I see in the dream they are someone's poems
to be wrested from an elliptic French.
A woman like me, her lines heavy with lovers,
locked churches, Saturday traffic jams.
When we meet on a park bench
in the Tuileries' frame I discover
her face is narrow and shy,
a nuthatch's, perhaps, tinted blue.
She runs headfirst down an ash tree.

Meanwhile her high heels click.
Her eyes are elusive, all-seeing,
her thighs fishlike,
her dress stressed at the seams.
My words wear the vapid smiles of cows
grazing along the text
on Alps of edelweiss.

I collapse her poems like rows
of chairs arranged for cheap funerals,
saying, see here, my friend,
my double, let us breathe
mouth to mouth like a lifesaving class
as chockful and as brave
forcefeeding each other's stopped lungs
so that at the feast of words
there will be no corpse to carve.

The Faint-Hearted Suicide

Where the arm
narrows down to its human part
where the skin
goes smooth as old beach glass
and ten underground thongs
tie the palm in place
tie the thumb
that squat wise man
in position

there at that gentle confluence
two worms
not exactly twins
sleep in their white welts
sleep ragged but uncurled
under the scars
where X marks the spot.

I finger it left to right.
I have it by heart
that white night:

the bathroom bulb a hot eye
the square white tiles
heaving against you
the shower rail dripping teeth
life at your temples
setting the time bomb
while the helpless towels
huddle in a corner
and the brand-new Wilkinson blade
winks out of the razor.

I think of the sweet streets
of your childhood—
Upsal, Tulpehocken, Queen's Lane—
an alphabet of old place names
tucked into your bicycle.

I think of those summer nights
spread wide as a platter
with the trumpet vines drowsing
their way up the veranda
and the porch swing a scratchy flute
answering the cicadas.

There was a bed made for you
there was a durable kitchen
there were waxed newel posts
footsteps that listened and loved you
and then
you had no way to
get back inside the geography.
No telegraph to tap out on
no one to cry uncle to.
The rented walls of Manhattan
locked arms to fence you
into Red Rover.

Two clean cuts
and the invited blood comes naked
comes slippery and abundant
a letting useful as leeches
bringing you back to your body
that boyhood
that kingdom.

from
THE AMANDA POEMS

Amanda Is Shod

The way the cooked shoes sizzle
dropped in a pail of cold water
the way the coals in the portable forge
die out like hungry eyes
the way the nails go in aslant
each one the tip of a snake's tongue

and the look of the parings
after the farrier's knife
has sliced through.

I collect them
four marbled white C's
as refined as petrified wood
and dry them to circles of bone
and hang them away on my closet hook

lest anyone cast a spell on Amanda.

This morning Amanda
lies down during breakfast.
The hay is hip high.
The sun sleeps on her back
as it did on the spine
of the dinosaur
the fossil bat
the first fish with feet
she was once.
A breeze fans
the deerflies from lighting.
Only a gaggle of gnats
housekeeps in her ears.
A hay plume sticks out of her mouth.

I come calling with a carrot
from which I have taken
the first bite.
She startles
she considers rising
but retracts the pistons
of her legs and accepts
as loose-lipped as a camel

We sit together.
In this time and place
we are heart and bone.
For an hour
we are incorruptible.

The Agnostic Speaks to Her Horse's Hoof

Come, frog, reveal yourself.
Surface out of the poultice
the muck and manure pack.
Make your miraculous V to stand up.
Show me as well the tickle place
that cleft between.

The Good Book says a man's life
is as grass the wind passes over
and is gone.
According to the *National Geographic*
the oceans will lie down dead
as cesspools in sixty years.

Let us ripen in our own way—
I with my back to the trunk
of a butternut that has caught
the fatal red canker
and on my knee
this skillet of your old foot.

The hoofpick is God's instrument
as much as I know of Him.

In my hands let it raise
your moon, Amanda, your nerve bone.
Let us come to the apocalypse complete
without splinter or stone.
Let us ride out
on four iron feet.

At night Amanda's eyes
are rage red with toy worlds inside.
Head on they rummage the dark
of the paddock like twin cigars
but flicker at the edges with
the shyer tongues of the spirit lamp.

There's little enough for her to see:
my white shirt, the sleeves
rolled high, two flaps of stale bread
in my fish paws. I can't sleep.
I have come back from
the feed-bag-checkered restaurant
from the pale loose tears of my dearest friend
her blue eyes sinking into the highball glass
her eyeballs clinking on ice
and her mouth drawn down in the grand
comedy of anguish.

Today a sparrow has been put
in the hawk's hands and in the net
a monarch crazes its wings on gauze.
A doe run down by the dogs
commonly dies of fright before
its jugular opens at the fang hole.
In my friend's eyes, hunger
holds an empty rice bowl.

O Amanda, burn out my dark.
Press the warm suede of your horseflesh
against my cold palm.
Take away all that is human.

The Summer of the Watergate Hearings

I wake in New Hampshire.
The sun is still withheld.
For six days Amanda has stood
through drizzles and downpours.

This morning she steams.
Little pyramids of her droppings
surround her. Dead worms
shine in them like forgotten

spaghetti, proof she has eaten
the sugar-coated cure.
Four dozen ascarids, ten strongyles—
I count them to make sure.

And all the while in Washington
worms fall out of the government
pale as the parasites that drain
from the scoured gut of my mare.

They blink open on the television screen.
Night after night on the re-run
I count them to make sure.

Consider Amanda, my sensible strawberry roan,
her face with its broad white blaze
lending an air of constant surprise.
Homely Amanda, colossal and mild.
She evokes those good ghosts of my childhood
brillo-haired and big-boned,
the freckled maiden aunts.
Though barren like her, they were not petulant.

Peaceable dears, they lay down alone
mute as giraffes in my mother's house,
fed tramps on the back porch
after The Crash,
pantomimed the Charleston
summer nights in the upstairs back bedroom
and dropped apple peels over their shoulders
to spell the name of a marrying man.

Remembering this,
I bring Amanda windfalls.
That season again.
The power of the leaf runs the human brain
raising the dead like lamb clouds in the sky.

The power of the thorn holds the birds' late nests
now strung like laundry from the blackberry canes
where parts of Amanda recur.
Her body fuzz is stickered in the oriole cups.
Copper hairs from her tail hang the packages up.

All fall as I drop to the scalp of sleep
while the raccoons whistle
and the geese cough
and Amanda grows small in my head,
the powder streak of her face a blur
seventy pastures off,
the aunts return letting down their hair.
It hangs to the custard of Harriet's lap.

It tickles the spine of Alma's girdle
and the dream unwinds like a top.

In 4/4 time the way it was once
I am brushing the carrot frizz gone gray
a hundred ritual strokes one way,
a hundred ritual strokes the other.
We dance the old back-bedroom dance
that rattles the shakes of my mother's house
till Amanda jitters yanking her tether,
her eyes green holes in the dark, her blaze
a slice of moon looming at the gate
and the latch flies up on another night.

Amanda, you'll be going
to Alpo or to Gaines
when you run out of luck;
the flesh flensed from your bones
your mammoth rib cage rowing
away to the renderer's
a dry canoe on a truck

while I foresee my corpse
slid feet first into fire
light as the baker's loaf
to make of me at least
a pint of potash spoor.
I'm something to sweeten the crops
when the clock hand stops.

Amanda, us in the woods
miles from home, the ground
upending in yellow flutes
that open but make no sound.
Ferns in the mouth of the brute,
chanterelles in the woman's sack . . .
what do I want for myself
dead center, bareback
on the intricate harp of your spine?
All that I name as mine

with the sure slow oxen of words:
feed sacks as grainy as boards
that air in the sun. A boy
who is wearing my mother's eyes.
Garlic to crush in the pan.
The family gathering in.
Already in the marsh
the yearling maples bleed
a rich onrush. Time slips
another abacus bead.

Let it not stick in the throat
or rattle a pane in the mind.
May I leave no notes behind
wishful, banal or occult
and you, small thinker in
the immensity of your frame,
may you be caught and crammed
midmouthful of the best grain
when the slaughterer's bullet slams
sidelong into your brain.

From Up Country

ıe Hermit Wakes to Bird Sounds

He startles awake. His eyes are full of white light.
In a minute the sun will ooze into the sky.
Meanwhile, all the machines of morning start up.

The typewriter bird is at it again.
Her style is full of endearing hesitations.
The words, when they come, do so in
the staccato rush of a deceitful loveletter.

The sewing machine bird returns to the doddering elm.
Like Penelope, she rips out yesterday's stitches
only to glide up and down, front and back
reentering the same needle holes.

The bird who presides at the wellhouse primes the pump.
Two gurgles, a pause, four squeaks of the handle
and time after time a promise of water
can be heard falling back in the pipe's throat.

Far off the logging birds saw into heartwood
with rusty blades, and the grouse cranks up
his eternally unstartable Model T
and the oilcan bird comes with his liquid pock pock

to attend to the flinty clanks of the disparate parts
and as the old bleached sun slips into position
slowly the teasing inept malfunctioning
one-of-a-kind machines fall silent.

The Hermit Meets the Skunk

The hermit's dog skitters home
drunk with it once every fall,
the whites of his eyes marbled
from the spray and his tail tucked
tighter than a clamshell. He contracts
himself to a mouse under the hermit's bed.

The hermit unsticks him with a broom
and ties him outside to a tree.
He is a spotted dog, black rampant
on white. And as the hermit scrubs,
the white goes satiny with Lava soap,
the black brightens to a bootblack shine.
Next, a dose of tomato juice stains
the white like a razor cut under water
and purples the black, and after that
the whole dog bleaches mooncolored
under a drench of cornstarch.
The hermit sniffs him. Skunk
is still plain as a train announcement.

So he is to be washed again,
rinsed again, powdered again
until the spots wink out again
under the neutral white.
Inside his mouth, the hermit knows
and knows from what is visible
under the tail, Dog is equally spotted
but in the interior, gray on a pink field.
If he were to be pinned down,
his four legs held at four corners,
and slit open by the enthusiast,
the hermit knows the true nature of Dog
spotted layer by layer
would be laid bare.

Afterward all night
skunk sleepwalks the house.

Skunk is a pot of copper pennies
scorched dry on a high flame.
Skunk is a porridge of dead shrews
stewed down to gelatin.
Skunk is the bloat of chicken gut
left ten days to sweeten in the sun.
Skunk is the mother bed, the ripe taste
of carrion, the green kiss.

The Hermit Prays

I hold in my hand this cup
this ritual, this slice of womb
woven of birchbark strips
and the woolly part of a burst cocoon
all mortared with mud and chinked
with papers of snakeskin.

I hold in my hand this carcass
this wintered-over thing.

What they are made of, these string
sacks, these tweezered and gluey cells
can only be said of a house,
of plumb bobs and carpenters' awls.

God of the topmost branch
god of the sheltering leaf
fold your wing over.
Keep secret and keep safe.

The Hermit Picks Berries

At midday the birds doze.
So does he.

The frogs cover themselves.
So does he.

The breeze holds its breath in the poplars.
Not one leaf turns its back.
He admires the stillness.

The snake uncoils its clay self
in the sun on a rock in the pasture.
It is the hermit's pasture.
He encourages the snake.

At this hour a goodly number
of blueberries decide to ripen.
Once they were wax white.
Then came the green of small bruises.
After that, the red of bad welts.
All this time they enlarged themselves.
Now they are true blue.

The hermit whistles as he picks.
Later he will put on his shirt
and walk to town for some cream.

The Hermit Goes Up Attic

An Englishman went to India to make a fortune first, in order that he might return England and live the life of a poet. He should have gone up garret at once.
—Thoreau, Walden

Up attic, Lucas Harrison, God rest
his frugal bones, once kept a tidy account
by knifecut of some long-gone harvest.
The pine was new. The pitch ran down to blunt
the year: 1811, the score: 10, he carved
into the center rafter to represent
his loves, beatings, losses, hours, or maybe
the butternuts that taxed his back and starved
the red squirrels higher up each scabbed tree.
1812 ran better. If it was bushels he risked,
he would have set his sons to rake them ankle deep
for wintering over, for wrinkling off their husks
while downstairs he lulled his jo to sleep.

By 1816, whatever the crop goes sour.
Three tallies cut by the knife is all
in a powder of dead flies and wood dust pale as flour.
Death, if it came then, has since grown dry and small.

But the hermit makes this up. Nothing is sure
under this rooftree keel veed in
with rafter ribs. Up here he always hears
the ghosts of Lucas Harrison's jackpines
complain, chafing against their mortised pegs,
a woman in childbirth pitching from side to side
until the wet head crowns between her legs
again, and again she will bear her man astride
and out of the brawl of sons he will drive like oxen
tight at the block and tackle, whipped to the trace,
come up these burly masts, these crossties broken
from their growing and buttoned into place.

Whatever it was is now a litter of shells.
Even at noon the attic vault is dim.
The hermit carves his own name in the sill
that someone after will take stock of him.

he Hermit Has a Visitor

Once he puts out the light
moth wings on the window screen slow
and drop away like film lapping the spool
after the home movie runs out.

He lies curled like a lima bean
still holding back its cotyledon.
Night is a honeycomb.
Night is the fur on a blue plum.

And then she sings. She raises the juice.
She is a needle, he the cloth.
She is an A string, he the rosewood.
She is the thin whine at concert pitch.

She has the eggs and he the blood
and after she is a small
red stain on the wall
he will itch.

Creatures

See here the diving beetle is split
flat on the underside like a peachpit

and kindergarten blue the frail
biplanes of dragonflies touch head to tail

and water measurers on jury-rigged
legs dent the surface film and whirligigs

crowblack and paddlefooted spin clock-
wise and counter somehow locked

in circus circles and backswimmers all
trim as college racing shells

row trailing their four eyes upside down
and mayflies seek the undersides of stones

to squirt their eggs in rows as straight as corn
and only after clamber out to drown

and the pond's stillness nippled as if
by rain instead is pocked with life

and all, all except the black horseleech
let pass my entering pale enormous flesh.

The moving of stones, that sly jockeying thrust
takes place at night underground, shoulders first.

They bud in their bunkers like hydras. They puff
up head after head and allow them to drop off

on their own making quahogs, cow flops, eggs and knee
caps. In this way one stone can infuse a colony.

Eyeless and unsurprised they behave
in the manner of stones: swallow turnips, heave graves

rise up openmouthed into walls and from time
to time imitate oysters or mushrooms.

The doors of my house are held open by stones
and to see the tame herd of them hump their backbones

as cumbrous as bears across the pasture in
an allday rain is to believe for an afternoon

of objects that waver and blur
in some dark obedient order.

The Dreamer, the Dream

After the sleeper has burst his night pod
climbed up out of its silky holdings
the dream must stumble alone now
must mope in the hard eye of morning

in search of some phantom outcome
while on both sides of the tissue
the dreamer walks into the weather
past time in September woods in the rain

where the butternuts settle around him
louder than tears and in fact he comes
upon great clusters of honey mushrooms
breaking the heart of old oak

a hundred caps grotesquely piggyback
on one another, a caramel mountain
all powdered with their white spores
printing themselves in no notebook

and all this they do in secret
climbing behind his back
lumbering from their dark fissure
going up like a dream going on.

eans

. . . making the earth say beans instead of grass—this was my daily work.
                                                    —*Thoreau*, Walden

Having planted
that seven-mile plot
he came to love it
more than he had wanted.
His own sweat
sweetened it.
Standing pat
on his shadow
hoeing every noon
it came to pass
in a summer long gone
that Thoreau
made the earth say beans
instead of grass.

You, my gardener
setting foot
among the weeds
that stubbornly reroot
have raised me up
into hellos
expansive as
those everbearing rows.

Even without
the keepsake strings
to hold the shoots
of growing things
I know this much:
I say beans
at your touch.

Mud

You would think that the little birches
would die of that brown mouth sucking
and sucking their root ends.
The rain runs yellow.
The mother pumps in, pumps in
more than she can swallow.
All of her pockmarks spill over.
The least footfall
brings up rich swill.

The streams grow sick with their tidbits.
The trout turn up their long bellies.
The slugs come alive. An army
of lips works in its own ocean.
The boulders gape to deliver themselves.
Stones will be born of that effort.

Meanwhile the mother is sucking.
Pods will startle apart,
pellets be seized with a fever
and as the dark gruel thickens,
life will stick up a finger.

Woodchucks

Gassing the woodchucks didn't turn out right.
The knockout bomb from the Feed and Grain Exchange
was featured as merciful, quick at the bone
and the case we had against them was airtight,
both exits shoehorned shut with puddingstone,
but they had a sub-sub-basement out of range.

Next morning they turned up again, no worse
for the cyanide than we for our cigarettes
and state-store Scotch, all of us up to scratch.
They brought down the marigolds as a matter of course
and then took over the vegetable patch
nipping the broccoli shoots, beheading the carrots.

The food from our mouths, I said, righteously thrilling
to the feel of the .22, the bullets' neat noses.
I, a lapsed pacifist fallen from grace
puffed with Darwinian pieties for killing,
now drew a bead on the littlest woodchuck's face.
He died down in the everbearing roses.

Ten minutes later I dropped the mother. She
flipflopped in the air and fell, her needle teeth
still hooked in a leaf of early Swiss chard.
Another baby next. O one-two-three
the murderer inside me rose up hard,
the hawkeye killer came on stage forthwith.

There's one chuck left. Old wily fellow, he keeps
me cocked and ready day after day after day.
All night I hunt his humped-up form. I dream
I sight along the barrel in my sleep.
If only they'd all consented to die unseen
gassed underground the quiet Nazi way.

One Small Death in May

I will not sing the death of Dog
who lived a fool to please his king.
I will put him under the milkweed bloom
where in July the monarchs come
as spotted as he, as rampant, as enduring.

Turning To

Death
is what I always think of
in these connections.

We lie
ruffling mouth to mouth
making one shadow

two lukewarm frogs
content with the single wardrobe
of our skins

at home with our tongues
those lazy intelligent
lickers down

of gnat wing and fly gauze
and the pellets
of newly hatched darning needles.

We feed in spasms
at ease in a teacup
or Lake Erie

and like frogs
we are to be overturned
by any stone heaved in the puddle.

We are to be taken down straightway
by the hognosed snake
or snipped up to accommodate the heron.

Meanwhile
let us cast one shadow
in air or water

our mouths wide as saucers
our tongues at work in their tunnels
our shut eyes unimportant as freckles.

Let us turn to, until
the giant flashlight
comes down on us

and we are rammed home on the corkscrew gig
one at a time
and lugged off belly to belly.

Part

V.

For a Shetland Pony Brood Mare
Who Died in Her Barren Year

After bringing forth eighteen
foals in as many Mays
you might, old Trinket girl,
have let yourself be lulled
this spring into the green days
of pasture and first curl
of timothy. Instead,
your milk bag swelled again,
an obstinate machine.
Your long pale tongue
waggled in every feed box.
You slicked your ears back
to scatter other mares
from the salt lick.
You were full of winter burdocks
and false pregnancy.

By midsummer all the foals
had breached, except the ghost
you carried. In the bog
where you came down each noon
to ease your deer-thin hoofs in mud,
a jack-in-the-pulpit cocked
his overhang like a question mark.
We saw some autumn soon
that botflies would take your skin
and bloodworms settle
inside the cords and bands
that laced your belly,
your church of folded hands.

But all in good time, Trinket!
Was it something you understood?
Full of false pride
you lay down and died
in the sun,
all silken on one side,
all mud on the other one.

The Presence

Something went crabwise
across the snow this morning.
Something went hard and slow
over our hayfield.
It could have been a raccoon
lugging a knapsack,
it could have been a porcupine
carrying a tennis racket,
it could have been something
supple as a red fox
dragging the squawk and spatter
of a crippled woodcock.
Ten knuckles underground
those bones are seeds now
pure as baby teeth
lined up in the burrow.

I cross on snowshoes
cunningly woven from
the skin and sinews of
something else that went before.

They come forth with all four legs folded in
like a dimestore card table.
Their hides are watered silk.
As in blindman's buff they rise, unable
to know except by touch, and begin
to root from side to side in search of milk.

The stanchions hang empty. Straw beds the planks
that day. On that day they are left at will
to nuzzle and malinger
under the umbrella of their mothers' flanks
sucking from those four fingers
they were called forth to fill.

Immediately thereafter each is penned
narrowly and well, like a Strasbourg goose.
Milk comes on schedule in a nippled pail.
It is never enough to set them loose
from that birthday dividend
of touch. Bleating racks the jail.

Across the barn the freshened cows
answer until they forget who is there.
Morning and night, machinery
empties their udders. Grazing allows
them to refill. The hungry
calves bawl and doze sucking air.

The sponges of their muzzles pucker
and grow wet with nursing dreams.
In ten weeks' time the knacker
—the local slaughterer—will back his truck
against the ramp, and prodded to extremes
they will kick and buck

and enter
and in our time they will come forth for good
dead center
wrapped and labeled in a plastic sheet,
their perfect flesh unstreaked with blood
or muscle, and we will eat.

Watering Trough

Let the end of all bathtubs
be this putting out to pasture
of four Victorian bowlegs
anchored in grasses.

Let all longnecked browsers
come drink from the shallows
while faucets grow rusty
and porcelain yellows.

Where once our nude forebears
soaped up in this vessel
come, cows, and come, horses.
Bring burdock and thistle,

come slaver the scum of
timothy and clover
on the castiron lip that
our grandsires climbed over

and let there be always
green water for sipping
that muzzles may enter thoughtful
and rise dripping.

Hello, Hello Henry

My neighbor in the country, Henry Manley,
with a washpot warming on his woodstove,
with a heifer and two goats and yearly chickens,
has outlasted Stalin, Roosevelt and Churchill
but something's stirring in him in his dotage.

Last fall he dug a hole and moved his privy
and a year ago in April reamed his well out.
When the county sent a truck and poles and cable,
his daddy ran the linemen off with birdshot
and swore he'd die by oil lamp, and did.

Now you tell me that all yesterday in Boston
you set your city phone at mine, and had it ringing
inside a dead apartment for three hours
room after empty room, to keep yours busy.
I hear it in my head, that ranting summons.

That must have been about the time that Henry
walked up two miles, shy as a girl come calling,
to tell me he has a phone now, 264, ring two.
It rang one time last week—wrong number.
He'd be pleased if one day I would think to call him.

Hello, hello Henry? Is that you?

Night, the Paddock, Some Dreams

All the loud night cocooned
in my farmhouse bed I hear
stones knock, an owl begin,
and the snuffles of my mare

who sleeps in fits and starts
warily upright
under the buckshot stars.
Only with the first light

she goes ungainly down
folding her leg sticks in
to lie like some overgrown
dachshund-turned-dinosaur,

her neck important as
Victorian furniture,
her backbone ridged and strong
as the Seven Hills of Rome.

She chews in her sleep, she makes
it plain she dreams of me.
In dreams and truth I rake
cut clover, timothy
wound up in vetch, such sweets
as the acreage allows.

I also dream gaunt cows
heads down in their own dung
and crueler images:
the ribs of all my dears
picked famine dry and hung
for lesser foragers.

Far worse than dreams go on.
Leave people out of this.
Let the loud night be gone
and may the old mare rouse
from dampness in her bones
and safely browse.

Country House

After a long presence of people,
after the emptying out,
the laying bare,
the walls break into conversation.
Their little hairlines ripple
and an old smile
crosses the chimney's face.

The same flies
drawn to the windowpanes
buzz endlessly from thirst.
Field mice coast down
a forgotten can of bacon fat.
Two clocks tick themselves witless.
October, clutching its blankets,
sidles from room to room
where the exhausted doors
now speak to their stops,
four scrubbed stones of common quartz.

They are gone,
those hearty moderns who came in
with their plastic cups and spoons
and restorative kits
for stripping the woodwork,
torn between making over
and making do.
At their leavetaking
the thin beds exhale.
The toilet bowl blinks,
its eye full of purple antifreeze.

As after a great drought
the earth opens its holes
to raise the water table,
the stairs undo their buttons.
The risers, each an individual,
slip out of plumb.

Seams, pores and crazings unpucker
making ready for frost.
A tongue of water
circles the cellar wall
and locks itself in.

Soon the raccoon will come
with his four wise hands
to pick the carcass
and the salt-worshiping porcupine
will chew sweat from the porch swing.
The red squirrels will decamp,
the last litter of mice go under.
Caught and fastened, this house
will lean into the January blizzard
letting its breath go sour,
its rib cage stiffen.

Making the Jam Without You

for Judy

Old daughter, small traveler
asleep in a German featherbed
under the eaves in a postcard town
of turrets and towers,
I am putting a dream in your head.

Listen! Here it is afternoon.
The rain comes down like bullets.
I stand in the kitchen,
that harem of good smells
where we have bumped hips and
cracked the cupboards with our talk
while the stove top danced with pots
and it was not clear who did
the mothering. Now I am
crushing blackberries
to make the annual jam
in a white cocoon of steam.

Take it, my sleeper. Redo it
in any of your three
languages and nineteen years.
Change the geography.
Let there be a mountain,
the fat cows on it belled
like a cathedral. Let
there be someone beside you
as you come upon the ruins
of a schloss, all overgrown
with a glorious thicket,
its brambles soft as wool.
Let him bring the buckets
crooked on his angel arms
and may the berries, vaster
than any forage in
the mild hills of New Hampshire,

drop in your pail, plum size,
heavy as the eyes
of an honest dog
and may you bear them
home together to a square
white unreconstructed kitchen
not unlike this one.

Now may your two heads
touch over the kettle,
over the blood of the berries
that drink up sugar and sun,
over that tar-thick boil
love cannot stir down.
More plainly than
the bric-a-brac of shelves
filling with jelly glasses,
more surely than
the light driving through them
trite as rubies, I see him
as pale as paraffin beside you.
I see you cutting
fresh baked bread to spread it
with the bright royal fur.

At this time
I lift the flap of your dream
and slip out thinner than a sliver
as your two mouths open
for the sweet stain of purple.

For My Son on the Highways
of His Mind

for Dan

Today the jailbird maple in the yard
sends down a thousand red hands in the rain.
Trussed at the upstairs window I
watch the great drenched leaves flap by
knowing that on the comely boulevard
incessant in your head you stand again
at the cloverleaf, thumb crooked outward.

Dreaming you travel light
guitar pick and guitar
bedroll sausage-tight
they take you as you are.

They take you as you are
there's nothing left behind
guitar pick and guitar
on the highways of your mind.

Instead you come home with two cops, your bike
lashed to the back of the cruiser because
an old lady, afraid of blacks and boys
with hair like yours, is simon-sure you took
her purse. They search you and of course you're clean.
Later we make it into a family joke,
a poor sort of catharsis. It wasn't the scene

they made—that part you rather enjoyed—
and not the old woman whose money turned up next day
in its usual lunatic place under a platter
but the principle of the thing, to be toyed
with cat and mouse, be one mouse who got away
somehow under the baseboard or radiator
and expect to be caught again sooner or later.

Dreaming you travel light
guitar pick and guitar
bedroll sausage-tight
they take you as you are.

Collar up, your discontent goes wrapped
at all times in the flannel army shirt
your father mustered out in, wars ago,
the ruptured duck still pinned to the pocket flap
and the golden toilet seat—the award his unit
won for making the bomb that killed the Japs—
now rubbed to its earliest threads, an old trousseau.

Meanwhile the posters on your bedroom wall
give up their glue. The corners start to fray.
Belmondo, Brando, Uncle Ho and Che,
last year's giants, hang lop-eared but hang on.
The merit badges, the model airplanes, all
the paraphernalia of a simpler day
gather dust on the shelf. That boy is gone.

They take you as you are
there's nothing left behind
guitar pick and guitar
on the highways of your mind.

How it will be tomorrow is anyone's guess.
The *Rand McNally* opens at a nudge
to forty-eight contiguous states, easy
as a compliant girl. In Minneapolis
I see you drinking wine under a bridge.
I see you turning on in Washington, D.C.,
panhandling in New Orleans, friendless

in Kansas City in an all-night beanery
and mugged on the beach in Venice outside L.A.
They take your watch and wallet and crack your head
as carelessly as an egg. The yolk runs red.
All this I see, or say it's what I see
in leaf fall, in rain, from the top of the stairs today
while your maps, those sweet pastels, lie flat and ready.

Dreaming you travel light
guitar pick and guitar
bedroll sausage-tight
they take you as you are.

They take you as you are
there's nothing left behind
guitar pick and guitar
on the highways of your mind.

he Fairest One of All

for Jane

Pirouettes of you are in order.
There ought to be slithers of satin
and diamonds buckled to your ears
and gold ropes cunningly knotted
under your breasts. A series of mirrors
ought to repeat your bare shoulders
while someone quite gravely
sprinkles rosin on the parquet floor
and the orchestra adjusts itself
to one violin's clear A.
Outside the casement windows
a late snow could set about filling
birds' nests, bee cells and the tines
of apple trees. If there are horses
now let them draw troikas
with bells made of brass to speak harshly
and let the middle-aged queen rap
asking her question.
All this ought to befall.

But in fact it does not. It is summer
in a room smelling of oranges and sweat
the upstairs spare room you live in
when you come home to visit.
You stand here ironing among the suitcases
the jodhpurs, tampons, ski boots
among the A. A. Milne, the dust-freckled
glass animals and the one-eyed fake bear rug.
Ironing in sunlight you put me
in mind of an aspen in August
all silverbacked leaf hands, slicking
one seam from wrist to shoulder
parting nine pleats with the hot metal nose
and closing them crisp as a lettuce cup.
You stand in an acre of whiteness

a sweet bending tree, a popple
with hands that kiss, smack, fold, tuck.

So far so good, my darling, my fair
first born, your hair black as ebony
your lips red as blood. But let there be
no mistaking how the dark scheme runs.
Too soon all this will befall:
Too soon the huntsman will come.
He will bring me the heart of a wild boar
and I in error will have it salted and cooked
and I in malice will eat it bit by bit
thinking it yours.
And as we both know, at the appropriate moment
I will be consumed by an inexorable fire
as you look on.

A son
is a monument,
the Stonehenge, the Easter Island
of a man's intent,
a noose
to catch the name and spin
it loose across
tomorrow to go on:
That is a son.

But in praise of daughters first there is
the matter of their comeliness,
the whole sweet smell of the house that holds them,
the tropic disorder that they bring,
the bright sherbet of their underwear dripdrying
and the cargo of their redemptive creams
that stain the bathroom porcelain
with the ooze of crushed flowers.
In praise of daughters!

I have not said there is the season
of tantrums when the throats of doors are cut
with cold slammings. Rooms fill with tears.
The bedclothes drown in blood
for these will be women. They will lie down
with lovers, they will cry out giving birth,
they will grow old with hard knuckles and dry necks.
Death will punish them with subtractions.
They will burn me and put me into the earth.

But today they come in the hour of their perfect skin
strict at the waist, hummocking at the thighs.
The kitchen bellies with the yeast
of their milky hands. The oven exhales
a bulge of apple and clove, and the ceiling
observes the agitation of their putting to rights.
They tickle the dog out of his middle age.
They unpaste memories like snapshots: *o remember?*
until the vintage cluster glistens.

They are
woodsmoke, bee balm, heartsease
my two girls
concise as cats
fastidious as pearls
and of them I sing in praise
whereas, my son,
you are my monument, my stone.
You go on.

You with the beard as red as Barbarossa's
uncut from its first sprouting to the hour
they tucked it in your belt and closed your eyes,
you with the bright brass water pipe, a surefire
plaything under the neighbors' children's noses
for you to puff and them to idolize

—the pipe you'd packed up out of somewhere
in Bohemia, along with the praying shawl
and the pair of little leather praying boxes—
Great-Grandfather, old blue-eyed fox of foxes,
I have three pages of you. That is all.

1895. A three-page letter
from Newport News, Virginia, written
on your bleached-out bills of sale under the stern
heading: ROSENBERG THE TAILOR, DEBTOR,
A FULL LINE OF GOODS OF ALL THE LATEST IN
SUITING AND PANTS. My mother has just been born.

You write to thank your daughter for the picture
of that sixth grandchild. There are six more to come.
"My heart's tenderest tendrils" is your style.
"God bless you even as He blessed Jacob." Meanwhile
you stitch the year away in Christendom.

Meanwhile it seems you've lost your wife, remarried
a girl your daughter's age and caused distress.
"It was a cold relentless hand of Death
that scattered us abroad," you write, "robbing us
of Wife and Mother." Grieving for that one buried
you send new wedding pictures now herewith
and close with *mazel* and *brocha,* words that bless.

The second bride lived on in one long study
of pleats and puckers to the age of ninety-two,

smoked cigarettes, crocheted and spoke of you
to keep our kinship threaded up and tidy.

Was that the message—the erratic ways
the little lore that has been handed on
suffers, but sticks it out in the translation?
I tell you to my children, who forget,
are brimful of themselves, and anyway
might have preferred a farmer or a sailor,
but you and I are buttoned, flap to pocket.
Welcome, ancestor, Rosenberg the Tailor!
I choose to be a lifetime in your debt.

Love, we are a small pond.
In us yellow frogs take the sun.
Their legs hang down. Their thighs open
like the legs of the littlest children.
On our skin waterbugs suggest incision
but leave no marks of their strokes.
Touching is like that. And what touch evokes.

Just here the blackest berries fatten
over the pond of our being.
It is a rich month for putting up weeds.
They jut like the jaws of Hapsburg kings.
Tomorrow they will drop their blood
as the milkweed bursts its cotton
leaving dry thorns and tight seeds.

Meanwhile even knowing
that time comes down to shut the door
—headstrong, righteous, time hard at the bone
with ice and one thing more—
we teem, we overgrow. The shelf
is tropic still. Even knowing
that none of us can catch up with himself

we are making a run
for it. Love, we are making a run.

After Love

Afterwards, the compromise.
Bodies resume their boundaries.

These legs, for instance, mine.
Your arms take you back in.

Spoons of our fingers, lips
admit their ownership.

The bedding yawns, a door
blows aimlessly ajar

and overhead, a plane
singsongs coming down.

Nothing is changed, except
there was a moment when

the wolf, the mongering wolf
who stands outside the self

lay lightly down, and slept.

he Lovers Leave by Separate Planes

She is going back
to the cash register of an old marriage.
He sees her ringing up days
letting the drawer fly open
on her half grown sons
and breaking the rolls of nickels and dimes
into their proper dividers
those easy rituals.

She thinks of him tomorrow at his desk
exploring an old translation
prying apart the brittle glue
between two languages to take out words.
She sees him lecturing gently to
an amphitheater of students
all of them taking useful notes
everyone gainfully occupied.

Meanwhile the lovers move apart
going east and west where they belong.
They have climbed in the same sky
to coast over clouds that loom
as solid as the Arctic Pole.
Whole counties of ice floes
are underfoot. At this point
the appearance of polar bears
would not surprise him
one holding a walleyed fish in its paws
one chewing the flipper of a stranded seal.

For that matter she is prepared
to see him well booted and fur capped
icicles in his beard
striding over the snowfield
as in a Bergman movie
breaking through gauze and violet gels
running abreast to knock at her window.

They would tell each other.
They would speak in large gestures
like deaf mutes
keeping nothing inside.

t the End of the Affair

That it should end in an Albert Pick hotel
with the air conditioner gasping like a carp
and the bathroom tap plucking its one-string harp
and the sourmash bond half gone in the open bottle,

that it should end in this stubborn disarray
of stockings and car keys and suitcases,
all the unfoldings that came forth yesterday
now crammed back to overflow their spaces,

considering the hairsbreadth accident of touch
the nightcap leads to—how it protracts
the burst of colors, the sweetgrass of two tongues,
then turns the lock in Hilton or in Sheraton,
in Marriott or Holiday Inn for such
a man and woman—bearing in mind these facts,

better to break glass, sop with towels, tear
snapshots up, pour whiskey down the drain
than reach and tangle in the same old snare
saying the little lies again.

Whippoorwill

It is indecent of this bird
to sing at night and
leave no shadow.
I flap up out of sleep
from some uncertain place
dragging my baggage:
a torn pillow, a tee-shirt
and a braided whip.

O Will, Billy, William
wherever you are and
under whatever name
this doleful bird must tell me
one hundred and forty-six times
the same story. It is
full of fear. Such shabbiness
in those three clear tones!
Pinched lips, missed chances,
runaways, loves you treated badly,
a room full of discards,
I among them.

Now the moon sits
on the window sill, one hip
humped like an Odalisque.
In that cold light the bird
tells me and tells me.
He cannot help it, Will.
Wherever we are he sings us
backward to the old bad times.
I too am a discard
and you,
you stick in his throat.

he Nightmare Factory

these are the dream machines
the dream machines
they put black ants in your bed
silverfish in your ears
they raise your father's corpse
they stick his bones in your sleep
or his stem or all thirty-two
of his stainless steel teeth
they line them up
like the best orchestra seats

these are the nightmare tools
down the assembly line
they send an ocean of feces
you swim in and wake from
with blood on your tongue
they build blind sockets
of subways and mine pits
for you to stop in
the walls slick as laundry soap
swelling and shrinking

these are the presses
they hum in nine languages
sing to the orphans
who eat pins for supper
the whole map of europe
hears the computers click
shunting the trains you take
onto dead sidings
under a sky that is
packed full of blackbirds

night after night in
the bowels of good citizens
nazis and cossacks ride
klansmen and judases

postmen with babies
stuffed in their mailsacks
and for east asians
battalions of giants
dressed in g i fatigues
ears full of bayonets

here on the drawing board
fingers and noses
leak from the air brush
maggots lie under
if i should die before
if i should die
in the back room
stacked up in smooth boxes
like soapflakes or tunafish
wait the undreamt of

Part

VI.

Morning Swim

Into my empty head there come
a cotton beach, a dock wherefrom

I set out, oily and nude
through mist, in chilly solitude.

There was no line, no roof or floor
to tell the water from the air.

Night fog thick as terry cloth
closed me in its fuzzy growth.

I hung my bathrobe on two pegs.
I took the lake between my legs.

Invaded and invader, I
went overhand on that flat sky.

Fish twitched beneath me, quick and tame.
In their green zone they sang my name

and in the rhythm of the swim
I hummed a two-four-time slow hymn.

I hummed "Abide With Me." The beat
rose in the fine thrash of my feet,

rose in the bubbles I put out
slantwise, trailing through my mouth.

My bones drank water; water fell
through all my doors. I was the well

that fed the lake that met my sea
in which I sang "Abide With Me."

Sisyphus

When I was young and full of shame
I knew a legless man who came

inside a little cart, inchmeal,
flatirons on his hands, downhill.

Under the railroad bridge his chant
singsonged all day *repent, repent*

for Jesus. On the way to school
I spoke to him to save my soul

and coming back, he made me stop
to count the nickels in his cap.

Eyes level with my petticoat
he whined to me. I smelled his goat-

smell, randy, thick, as brown as blood.
I did the only thing I could.

I wheeled my master up the hill.
I rolled him up as he sat still.

Up past the sisters of Saint Joe
I pushed my stone so God would know.

And he, who could not genuflect
on seamy stumps, stitched his respect

with fingers in the air. He called
me a perfect Christian child.

One day I said I was a Jew.
I wished I had. I wanted to.

The basket man is gone; the stone
I push uphill is all my own.

The symbol inside this poem is my father's feet
which, after fifty years of standing behind
the counter waiting on trade,
were tender and smooth and lay on the ironed sheet,
a study of white on white, like a dandy's shirt.
A little too precious; custom-made.
At the end of a day and all day Sunday they hurt.
Lying down, they were on his mind.

The sight of his children barefoot gave him a pain
—part anger, part wonder—as sharp as gravel
inside his lisle socks.
Polacks! he said, but meant it to mean
hod carriers, greenhorns, peasants; not ghetto Poles
once removed. *Where are your shoes? In hock?*
I grew up under the sign of those three gold balls
turning clockwise on their swivel.

Every good thing in my life was secondhand.
It smelled of having been owned before me by
a redcap porter whose ticket
ran out. I saw his time slip down like sand
in the glass that measured our breakfast eggs. At night
he overtook me in the thicket
and held me down and beat my black heart white
to make the pawnbroker's daughter pay.

On Saturday nights the lights stayed lit until ten.
There were cops outside on regular duty to let
the customers in and out.
I have said that my father's feet were graceful and clean.
They hurt when he turned the lock
on the cooks and chauffeurs and unlucky racetrack touts
and carwash attendants and laundresses and stock-
room boys and doormen in epaulets;

they hurt when he did up accounts in his head
at the bathroom sink

of the watches, cameras, typewriters, suitcases, guitars,
cheap diamond rings and thoroughbred
family silver, and matched them against the list
of hot goods from Headquarters,
meanwhile nailbrushing his knuckles and wrists
clean of the pawn-ticket stains of purple ink.

Firsthand I had from my father a love ingrown
tight as an oyster, and returned it
as secretly. From him firsthand
the grace of work, the sweat of it, the bone-
tired unfolding down from stress.
I was the bearer he paid up on demand
with one small pearl of selfhood. Portionless,
I am oystering still to earn it.

Not of the House of Rothschild, my father, my creditor
lay dead while they shaved his cheeks and blacked his mustach
My lifetime appraiser, my first prince whom death unhorsed
lay soberly dressed and barefoot to be burned.
That night, my brothers and I forced
the cap on his bottle of twenty-year-old Scotch
and drank ourselves on fire beforehand
for the sacrament of closing down the hatch,

for the sacrament of easing down the ways
my thumb-licking peeler of cash on receipt of the merchandise
possessor of miracles left unredeemed on the shelf
after thirty days,
giver and lender, no longer in hock to himself,
ruled off the balance sheet,
a man of great personal order
and small white feet.

Hungry for oysters to suck down with gin
we go at sunset and low water when
the sea returns our backyard, scrubbed but stinking.
In an abundance of dying, crabs bleach out
their whiskery legs, and fields of minnows
stiffen like orderly sardines, their eyes intact.
The shell of a horseshoe crab is the Kaiser's helmet
I swing by the tail till the natural glue lets go.

We walk in the shallows where stones become oysters
older than stones, grown in on each other
lip over lip, greasy with algae, to cover
the eyeball we eat. Until we unlock the joints,
alive. Alive, perhaps, as we swallow.
Now they belong to the stones. Standing on stones,
we are the oyster killers who live in a world
of sundown and gin and shellfish within our means.

At night the sound of water rocks our bed.
The chowder moon is a bowl of milky clams.
And as we lie in a tangle of stars and pines,
hardshell beetles blunder against the screen,
roll on their backs and die, cracking like popcorn.

By the hall light that pulls the June bugs down,
I see your legs walk past me to the window.
Your buttocks are two moons tipped on their cradles.
Your back, a new tent arching. Snakes sit
in the bulge of your arms, their tongues your elbows.

The big bed smells of salt. When you come back,
I move from my own cocoon to wind in yours.
Inside my eyes I count the shapes of shells:
the armor of broken beetles, mismatched halves
of oysters, the calico tops of scalded crabs,
and fishes' eyes, a thousand empty windows.
I will not count our own small gift of bones.
We hold ourselves in one world at a time.

The Widow

I latch the storm door, shunt the cat
down cellar, set the thermostat

and climb twelve steps to go to bed
myself, myself. I fold the spread.

The sheets are crisp. All over town
the yellow mouths of bedrooms yawn

and close on lovers, two by two.
I stuff the noisy door, undo

my buttons, hooks and eyes and stand
back from the mirror. Under hands

that mapped my senses softly as sheep
touch in the fold and turn in sleep

my body turned in appetite.
My jailbird body, long and light,

unfingermarked, unvisited,
grows stupid in the tidy bed.

Now as I turn the clock face down
midnight strikes all over town.

The Appointment

This is my wolf. He sits
at the foot of the bed
in the dark all night

breathing so evenly
I am almost deceived.
It is not the swollen

cat uncurling
restlessly, a house
of kittens knocking

against her flanks;
it isn't the hot fog
fingering the window locks

while the daffodils
wait in the wings
like spearholders;

not the children fisted
in three busy dreams
they will retell at breakfast;

and not you, clearly
not you beside me
all these good years

that he watches.
I lie to him nightlong.
I delay him with praises.

In the morning we wash
together chummily.
I rinse my toothbrush.

After that,
he puts his red eyes out
under the extra blanket.

To an Astronaut Dying Young

Tell us: are you dead yet? The elephant ears of our radar
still read you, wobbling over our heads like a baby star.

They say you will orbit us now once every ninety minutes
for years. And nothing about you will rot in your climate.

Down here it is spring. Whole townships huddle outdoors in the evenir
round-eyed as the cattle once were, but this time watching and waving

as your little light winks overhead, as it tilts and veers to the west.
You sit in the contour chair that fitted your torso best

but by summer, who will still think to measure your perigee?
Only the faithful few who set up a rescue committee.

Such ingenuity! Think now; can God have invented it?
We know that when planes crack open and spill the unlucky ones out,

there are tag ends to go on. He stands by to pick up the pieces
we label, and grieving, hand back to His care at requiem masses.

Even the dead at sea have a special path to His bosom.
Combing the mighty waves, He grapples up souls from the bottom.

But there you go again, locked up in your perfect manhood,
coasting beyond the reach of the last seraph in the void.

Not one levitating saint can rise from the golden pavement
high enough over the ridgepole to yank you back into His tent.

This was a comfortable kingdom, the dome of it tastefully pearled
till you cut loose. Your kind of death is out of God's world.

Quarry, Pigeon Cove

The dead city waited,
hung upside down in the quarry
without leafmold or pondweed
or a flurry of transparent minnows.
Badlands the color of doeskin
lay open like ancient Egypt.

Frog fins strapped to my feet,
a teaspoon of my own spit in the mask
to keep the glass from fogging,
and the thumbsuck rubber air tube in my mouth,
I slid in on my stomach,
a makeshift amphibian.

Whatever the sky was doing
it did now on its own.
The sun shone for the first fifteen feet going down,
then flattened, then petered out.
I hung on the last rung of daylight,
breathing out silver ball bearings,
and looked for the square granite bottom.

I might have swum down looking
soundlessly into nothing,
down stairways and alleys of nothing
until the city took notice
and made me its citizen,
except that life stirred overhead.
I looked up. A dog walked over me.

A dog was swimming and splashing.
Air eggs nested in his fur.
The hairless parts of him bobbled like toys
and the silk of his tail blew past like milkweed.
The licorice pads of his paws
sucked in and out,
making the shapes of kisses.

After that,
the nap of the surface resettled.
Mites danced on both sides of it.
Coming up, my own face seemed beautiful.
The sun broke on my back.

I am fighting fiercely
for it by lying down,
but the Walden of my mind
fills up with berry pickers,
litterbugs, picnickers
with outsize children,
all the crying kind.

Actually, overlap
is my worst problem.

When the lines that I dangle
in Walden
are hauled in,
the tail of one thought
is found to be hooked
in the mouth of another
and that one
is equally firmly caught
by another of which I am not
especially fond,
and the endless flapping
of fishes ends by
swamping the pond.

But I digress,
making images out of sleeplessness.

Somewhere is Innisfree,
is Zion,
somewhere a womb
opens inward,
a kind whale whose stomach room
is warmly moist
and undangerously brown.
I am fighting fiercely
for it by lying down.

Prothalamion

The far court opens for us all July.
Your arm, flung up like an easy sail bellying,
comes down on the serve in a blue piece of sky
barely within reach, and you following
tip forward on the smash. The sun sits still
on the hard white linen lip of the net. Five-love.
Salt runs behind my ears at thirty-all.
At game I see the sweat that you're made of.
We improve each other, quickening so by noon
that the white game moves itself, the universe
contracted to the edge of the dividing line
you toe against, limbering for your service,
arm up, swiping the sun time after time,
and the square I live in, measured out with lime.

And suppose the darlings get to Mantua,
suppose they cheat the crypt, what next? Begin
with him, unshaven. Though not, I grant you, a
displeasing cockerel, there's egg yolk on his chin.
His seedy robe's aflap, he's got the rheum.
Poor dear, the cooking lard has smoked her eye.
Another Montague is in the womb
although the first babe's bottom's not yet dry.
She scrolls a weekly letter to her Nurse
who dares to send a smock through Balthasar,
and once a month, his father posts a purse.
News from Verona? Always news of war.
  Such sour years it takes to right this wrong!
  The fifth act runs unconscionably long.

Despair

is a mildewed tent. Under the center pole
you must either bend double or take to your knees.
And suppose, after all that tugging and smoothing, you ease
yourself, blind end first, into your blanket roll—
wet under, and over, wool scratch, and you lying still,
lashed down for the season, hands crossed between your thigh
the canvas stink in your nose, the night in your eyes—
what makes you think that rattling your ribs here will
save you? Camper, you are a bone-sore fool.
Somewhere a brown moth beats at a lighted window.
Somewhere a weasel fastens into his mouse.
The ground heaves up its secret muster of toadstools;
they are marching to bear you away to the dumb show.
Yank up the pegs and come back! Come back in the house.

anuary 25th

All night in the flue like a trapped thing,
like a broken bird,
the wind knocked unanswered.
Snow fell down the chimney, making
the forked logs spit
ashes of resurrected crickets.
By 3 a.m. both stoves were dead.
A ball of steel wool
froze to the kitchen window sill,
while we lay back to back in bed,

two thin survivors. Somewhere in a small dream,
a chipmunk uncorked from his hole
and dodged along the wall.
My love, we live at such extremes
that when, in the leftover spite of the storm,
we touch and grow warm,
I can believe I saw
the ground release
that brown and orange commonplace
sign of thaw.

Now daylight the color of buttermilk
tunnels through the coated glass.
Lie still; lie close.
Watch the sun pick
splinters from the window flowers.
Now under the ice, under twelve knee-deep layers
of mud in last summer's pond
the packed hearts of peepers are beating
barely, barely repeating
themselves enough to hang on.

May 10th

I mean
the fiddleheads have forced their babies,
blind topknots first, up from the thinking rhizomes
and the shrew's children, twenty to a teaspoon,
breathe to their own astonishment
in the peephole burrow.

I mean
a new bat hangs upside down in the privy;
its eyes are stuck tight, its wrinkled pink mouth twitches
and in the pond, itself an invented puddle,
tadpoles quake from the jello
and come into being.

I mean, walk softly.
The maple's little used-up bells are dropping
and the new leaves are now unpacking,
still wearing their dimestore lacquer,
still cramped and wet from the journey.

On this day of errors
a field mouse brings forth her young
in my desk drawer.

Come for a pencil,
I see each one,
a wet steel thimble pulled out of its case,
begin to worm its way uphill
to a pinhead teat.

As if I were an enlarged owl
made both gross and cruel,
I lean closer.

The mother rears and kills.
Her forelegs loop like paper clips
as she tears at her belly fur,
shredding it fine as onion skin,
biting the blind and voiceless nubbles off.

Later, she runs past me.
I see her mouth
is stuffed full of a dead baby.

Part VII.

alfway

As true as I was born into
my mother's bed in Germantown,
the gambrel house in which I grew
stood halfway up a hill, or down,
between a convent and a madhouse.

The nunnery was white and brown.
In summertime they said the mass
on a side porch, from rocking chairs.
The priest came early on the grass,
black in black rubbers up the stairs
or have I got it wrong? The mass
was from the madhouse and the priest
came with a black bag to his class
and ministered who loved him least.
They shrieked because his needles stung.
They sang for Christ upon His cross.
The plain song and the bedlam hung
on the air and blew across
into the garden where I played.

I saw the sisters' linens flap
on the clothesline while they prayed,
and heard them tell their beads and slap
their injuries. But I have got
the gardens mixed. It must have been
the mad ones who cried out to blot
the frightened sinner from his sin.
The nuns were kind. They gave me cake
and told me lives of saints who died
aflame and silent at the stake
and when I saw their Christ, I cried

where I was born, where I outgrew
my mother's bed in Germantown.
All the iron truths I knew
stood halfway up a hill, or down.

Fräulein Reads Instructive Rhymes

Outside Help for Parents Who May Have Forgotten "Der Struwelpeter"
by Heinrich Hoffmann.

First hear the story of Kaspar the rosy-cheeked.
Once he was round and fat. He ate his dinner up.
Then, see, on Monday night, nothing will Kaspar eat.
Tuesday and Wednesday, *nein!* Kaspar throws down his cup.
Watch him shrink to a stick crying *nicht!* all that week.
Sunday he whispers *nicht* and falls down dead.
Now they must bury him. In the black earth he's meek.
And by his grave they leave Kaspar his meat and bread.
    Therefore, says Fräulein, slicing the sauerbraten,
    eat what I fix for you. See what can happen?

Next prances Friedrich the terrible-tempered.
He pulls the wings from flies.
He wrings the chickens' necks.
See with a long horsewhip how in this picture he
lashes the maid who cries into her handkerchief.
Wait, *aber,* all is well. Here the big dog comes in.
Angry black dog bites his knee and holds fast.
Now the Herr Doktor pours Friedrich bad medicine.
Downstairs, the napkined dog eats Friedrich's liverwurst.
    Child, says Fräulein, clicking her thimble cup,
    good, *ja,* be good, or the dog comes to eat you up.

Now look at Konrad the little thumb-sucker.
Ach, but his poor mama cries when she warns him
the tailor will come for his thumbs if he sucks them.
Quick he can cut them off, easy as paper.
Out goes the mother and *wupp!* goes the thumbkin in.
Then the door opens. Enter the tailor.
See in the picture the terrible tongue in
his grinning red mouth! In his hands the great shears.
Just as she told him, the tailor goes *klipp und klapp.*
Eight-fingered Konrad has learned a sad lesson.
    Therefore, says Fräulein, shaking her chignon,
    suck you must not or the tailor will chop!

Here is smart Robert the flying boy, bad one.
Hui! How the storm blows and coughs in the treetops.
Mama has told him today he must stay in,
but Robert slips out with umbrella and rain cap.
Now he is flying. The wind sucks and pulls him.
See, he is carried up, smaller and smaller.
His cap flies ahead of him, no one can help him.

   Therefore, says Fräulein, smoothing her collar,
   mind me, says Fräulein. God stands up in Heaven.
   See how He watches? He snatches the bad ones.

400-Meter Free Style

THE GUN full swing the swimmer catapults and cracks
                                                    s
                                                    i
                                                    x
feet away onto that perfect glass he catches at
a
n
d
throws behind him scoop after scoop cunningly moving
                                                    t
                                                    h
                                                    e
water back to move him forward. Thrift is his wonderful
s
e
c
ret; he has schooled out all extravagance. No muscle
                                                    r
                                                    i
                                                    p
ples without compensation wrist cock to heel snap to
h
i
s
mobile mouth that siphons in the air that nurtures
                                                    h
                                                    i
                                                    m
at half an inch above sea level so to speak.
T
h
e
astonishing whites of the soles of his feet rise
                                                    a
                                                    n
                                                    d

salute us on the turns. He flips, converts, and is gone
a
l
l
in one. We watch him for signs. His arms are steady at
                                                        t
                                                        h
                                                        e
catch, his cadent feet tick in the stretch, they know
t
h
e
lesson well. Lungs know, too; he does not list for
                                                    a
                                                    i
                                                    r
he drives along on little sips carefully expended
b
u
t
that plum red heart pumps hard cries hurt how soon
                                                    i
                                                    t
                                                    s
near one more and makes its final surge   TIME: 4:25:9

Casablanca

As years unwind now reels unwind.
Gray springs out of the hair,
cheeks refill, and eyelids lighten.
Bogie, beautifully indifferent,
seduces a cigarette and womankind.

Ingrid, in perilous rain
intensified by angle shots,
is Juno, fair and fair.
Where France falls and gates clang shut
she faithfully misses the final train.

Now Vichy is dead, and Peter Lorre
less cowardly, and Greenstreet
has gone with the parrot,
and I knew a boy with sandy hair
could do the dialogue all blurry;

cigarette dangling, cheeks sucked hollow,
hands in his jacket pockets,
could do the dialogue
for drinks at any party;
went down with his destroyer, swallowed

in the other half of that real war.
The tough guy, lately dead
of cancer, holds the girl and then they kiss
for the last time, and time goes west
and we come back to where we really are.

Hundred Nights

Dark came first and settled in
the pin oak rubbing on my screen.
Ten lightning bugs sealed in a milk
jar on my bureau winked and sulked.
I washed into a dream of a hunchback
chasing me with an empty mail sack

until the terrible mouse with wings
notched like bread knives came skittering
down the chimney next to my bed;
rudderless, raving, flapped and shied
against the ceiling, bedclothes, table.
I screamed as soon as I was able.

Father in a union suit
came a hundred sultry nights,
came like an avenging ghost.
He waved a carpetbeater, trussed
with scrolls of hearts and cupid wings,
a racket with rococo strings.

Two uncles one floor up ran down
a hundred nights to cheer and groan
as Father swore and chipped the plaster,
a game he never cared to master.
My father had his principles.
He smacked to stun them, not to kill.

Frozen underneath the sheets,
I heard the bats mew when he hit.
I heard them drop like squashing fruit.
I heard him test them with his foot.
I knew when he unlatched the screen
and sent them skimming by one wing.

The fall revived them, so he said.
I cried. I wished that they were dead.
I begged him stuff the chimney stack.

I pinched my lips to stay awake
to keep those flapping rats outside,
sang to myself, told riddles, prayed.

I memorized those crepey nights
with dying fireflies for lights:
the heave of wings come down horn-mad
to thump and thwack against the shade.
No matter that my parents said
it only happened twice that way

and all the rest were in my head.
Once, before my father died,
I meant to ask him why he chose
to loose those furies at my bed.

This dwelt in me who does not know me now,
where in her labyrinth I cannot follow,
advance to be recognized, displace her terror;
I hold my heartbeat on my lap and cannot comfort her.
Tonight she is condemned to cry out wolf
or werewolf, and it echoes in the gulf
and no one comes to cradle cold Narcissus;
the first cell that divided separates us.

On Being Asked to Write a Poem for the Centenary of the Civil War

Good friend, from my province what is there to say?
My great-grandfather left me here
rooted in grateful guilt,
who came, an escaped conscript
blasted out of Europe in 1848;
came, mourned by all his kin
who put on praying hats
and sat a week on footstools there;
plowed forty days by schooner
and sailed in at Baltimore
a Jew, and poor;
strapped needles up and notions
and walked packaback across
the dwindling Alleghenies,
his red beard and nutmeg freckles
dusting as he sang.

There are no abolitionists in my past to point to.
The truth is that this man,
my only link with that event,
prospered in Virginia, begat
eight young and sewed eight years
on shirts to get them bread.
When those warm states stood up to fight,
the war made him a factory
in a pasture lot where he sat,
my part-time pacifist,
stitching uniforms for the Confederates.
The gray cloth made him rich;
they say he lived to lose it all.
I have only a buckle and a candlestick
left over, like old rhetoric,
from his days

to show how little I belong.
This is the way I remember it was told,
but in a hundred years
all stories go wrong.

The First Rain of Spring

This is the first rain of spring;
it is changing to snow in the west.
The children sleep, closing the ring;
this is the first rain of spring.
Darkly, inside the soft nest,
the children sleep, closing the ring,
knees flexed under the breast.
It is changing to snow in the west.

We store for death's fattening
the easeful seed in its caul.
It clasps and unclasps like a spring;
we store for death's fattening.
Feel it! The fist to the wall;
it clasps and unclasps like a spring,
mindless, habitual,
the easeful seed in its caul.

Days will expand to the west;
winter is over is all.
Darkly, inside the soft nest,
days will expand to the west.
Feel it! The fist to the wall;
we hoard for life's sweetening.
Winter is over is all.
The children sleep, closing the ring.

The Journey

for Jane at thirteen

Papers in order; your face
accurate and on guard in the cardboard house
and the difficult patois you will speak
half-mastered in your jaw;
the funny make-up in your funny pocketbook—
pale lipstick, half a dozen lotions
to save your cloudless skin
in that uncertain sea
where no one charts the laws—
of course you do not belong to me
nor I to you
and everything is only true in mirrors.

I help to lock your baggage:
history book, lace collar and pink pearls
from the five-and-ten,
an expurgated text
of how the gods behaved on Mount Olympus,
and pennies in your shoes.
You lean as bland as sunshine on the rails.
Whatever's next—
the old oncoming uses
of your new troughs and swells—
is coin for trading among girls
in gym suits and geometry classes.

How can you know I traveled here,
stunned, like you, by my reflection
in forest pools;
hunted among the laurel
and whispered to by swans
in accents of my own invention?

It is a dangerous time.
The water rocks away the timber

and here is your visa stamped :
You lean down yo..
We exchange
and wave you o..

ALBERTSON COLLEGE OF IDAHO
PS3521.U638.A6.1982b
Our ground time here will be brief /

3 5556 00074044 9

DEMCO, INC. 38-2931

224

DATE DUE JAN 1 6 1993

FE 10'93			
DE 6 '95			

PS
3521
U638
A6
1982b

141230

N.L. TERTELING LIBRARY
ALBERTSON COLLEGE
CALDWELL, IDAHO

PURCHASED WITH NEH
ENDOWMENT FUNDS